Lemon
Yellow
Lies

Lemon Yellow Lies

EMILY OBERTON

 Nolan Publishing
Company

Cover art by DLR Cover Designs

Internal images © Julien Eichinger/Adobe Stock; Tartila/Adobe Stock

Lemon Yellow Lies/ Emily Oberton. — 1st ed.

ISBN 978-1-7347003-1-2

For Miles

CHAPTER ONE

I didn't typically force my way through locked doors, and certainly not those belonging to clients.

Today, however, was an exception.

Pulling apart the long handles of the bolt cutters, I positioned the twin steel blades on either side of the padlock's rusty shackle. Cutting through locks was a skill set I didn't like to brag about. As an interior designer, it made for lousy résumé material and bred unnecessary trust issues.

"You grab the left handle, I'll grab the right," I told my new friend Erin, who stood next to me at the door to my client's backyard shed. "On the count of three, we'll push the handles together and see if we can pop this baby off the latch. One, two—"

We both started pushing, too eager to get inside the shed to wait for the count of three. Grunting and panting, thrusting and writhing, we strained to close the bolt cutters.

Breaking and entering was hard work.

There was a loud clank as the blades sliced through the shackle. I tossed the bolt cutters to the ground, removed the broken padlock and slid open the latch, then gripped the handle and lifted the roll-up door.

The thin metal curtain rumbled as it coiled around the overhead bar.

I nodded at Erin. "We're in."

Stepping inside the pool equipment shed, I surveyed its contents. Directly in front of me was the filtering unit, which sat next to the heater and a small pump.

Erin nudged my arm. "Hadley, look. In the corner."

I followed her gaze to a jumbled heap of pool floats.

"I call dibs on the pineapple!" she declared, lunging for the pile and grabbing the float. Erin ran past me and out of the shed. Seconds later there was a splash, followed by a squeal.

I browsed the medley of pool noodles and fruit-shaped floats. It made me smile to imagine my client, the charming Kent Reading, sunbathing in his pool on a giant strawberry. I also imagined how grateful he would be when I told him I'd removed his padlock and replaced it with a new one. Kent had misplaced the key to his old one and couldn't access the floats or, more importantly, pool equipment.

Deciding on the watermelon float, I pulled it from the pile and dragged it out to the pool. It was Thursday, and I'd been working diligently the past four days to furnish Kent's outdoor living space by Monday—all while he was in Philadelphia on a business trip. He was hosting a surprise birthday party for his fiancée in less than two weeks, and had decided at the last moment his backyard just wasn't good enough for her.

Kent had shown me photos of design styles he liked, but he didn't care to be involved in the selection of furnishings. He only had two requirements: provide enough outdoor seating for at least twenty people, and create a tropical oasis that would dazzle his fiancée.

In record time, I created 3D design renderings of the space, and after receiving Kent's two-word 'looks good' approval in an email, I found and ordered all of the furniture and decor. A contractor finished repainting the pool equipment shed yesterday, and the furniture was scheduled to arrive over the next two days. Everything was on track to finish by the time his fiancée returned from New York on Monday.

Now it was time to relax.

Lifting the pitcher of strawberry lemon mojitos I'd made, I filled my glass and topped off Erin's, then set them in a floating drink holder.

I dipped my toes into the pool. Despite the unseasonably warm early-March weather, the water was chilly. But I didn't want to pass up the opportunity to swim in Kent's resort-like pool to save myself from a few goosebumps.

I flopped onto the bright red watermelon float and tilted my face to the sky, soaking up every last delicious drop of the waning afternoon sun.

Palm trees lining the pool extended high above the backyard. Underneath the canopy of rustling fronds, everything was quiet and still. A natural stone cabana, complete with an outdoor kitchen, fireplace, and big-screen TV, sat between the pool and back of the house. The cabana had plenty of room for tables and chairs, but at the moment was empty. It was a blank slate, ready to be filled with all the new furnishings I'd ordered.

"This is the life, isn't it?" I said to Erin, who was splayed out on the inflatable pineapple. Reaching for the floating drink holder, I grabbed my strawberry lemon mojito and took a long sip.

"Yes, but unfortunately it isn't *my* life." Laughing, she flipped over onto her stomach and looked at me through thick-rimmed sunglasses. "Or yours."

I grinned. "It is for one week. Seven glorious days of pretending this house and pool are mine." I lived in New Orleans but traveled to Darlington Hills, a small town nestled in the middle of the Virginia Peninsula, last weekend for a job interview at Walnut Ridge Furniture and Decor, a popular online home furnishings company.

My interview ended up being postponed until Saturday, but I serendipitously snagged the redesign project during brunch on Sunday when I met Erin. She owned the Whisks and Whiskers Cat Café, which had delicious coffee and adorable cats running around that were available for adoption. Erin had introduced me to Kent, her boyfriend's boss, who asked if I was interested in taking on a small-scale project with a tight deadline.

Before I was even two-thirds the way finished with my vanilla latte and eggs benedict, Kent had hired me to not only redesign his patio, but also to stay at his house while he was out of town so I could work around the clock and take care of his dog.

I had planned to stay the week with my aunt, who lived on the west side of Darlington Hills, but the housesitting gig came with some appealing perks, like extra money and free use of his pool.

If nothing else, the project was a good way to pass the time before my interview on Saturday, which I was already nervous about. Getting hired at Walnut Ridge was a key step in my plan to move as quickly and as far away from New Orleans as possible. I was like a fugitive, running from a bad breakup and broken heart.

A car door slammed somewhere in the neighborhood and the poolside serenity was disrupted by high-pitched howling. It was Kent's little pouf ball Bichon dog, Chip, who stood rigid by the side of the water. Kent had said he couldn't board Chip because he was a nervous dog. Apparently by 'nervous' he meant profoundly anxious and high-strung. The poor dog got worked up whenever the microwave oven dinged.

Erin sat up on the float, fluffed her long blonde curls, and adjusted the strap of her barely there bikini. Erin was a year shy of forty and anything but shy in a swimsuit. Her toned tummy told me she did far less sampling of Whisks and Whiskers' sweet treats than I would do if I owned a café.

"That darn yipper-yapper can't go five minutes without fussing," she said, frowning at Chip. "This is why you won't find any dogs at Whisks and Whiskers. I'd have to change the name to Whisks and Whiners. Or Barks and Bites."

"How about Forks and Fleas?" I added, laughing.

Chip paused his howling and looked at me. As usual, one of his eyes was closed as though it had gotten stuck while winking.

"Chi-ip," I sang, stretching his name into multiple syllables. "Calm down, boy. Everything's fine."

The back door to the house opened and a tall young woman stepped outside. She wore a corporate-esque pantsuit and had a bright yellow dress slung over her forearm. Chip turned his nose to the sky and resumed howling.

"Chip! Get back inside," the woman shouted. "How did you get out—" She froze when she saw me. "Who are you? What are you doing here?"

I considered asking her the same questions, but the keys dangling from her pinkie finger told me she'd probably let herself in legally.

"What's going on?" she demanded. You two are trespassing on private property. I'm calling the police if you don't explain why you're in Kent's pool on *my* floats."

"I'm Hadley Sutton with Hadley Home Design," I said, using the most chipper, non-criminal sounding voice I could summon. Even though we had a perfectly legitimate reason for being in Kent's backyard, I didn't want the police to come out. Talk about a bad first impression among locals and potential clients. If I moved to Darlington Hills, I wanted to start out with a clean reputation and police record. "Kent hired me to redesign his outdoor patio."

The woman lifted her eyebrows. "I'm Marian Koh, Kent's fiancée."

"Oh! You're back early," I said. "Kent told me you would return on Monday."

I glanced at the yellow dress draped over her arm. It made sense she was his fiancée. Kent had asked me to include yellow accents throughout the patio area because it was her favorite color. Per his guidance, I was incorporating multiple splashes of yellow around the pool area: patio sun umbrellas, throw pillows for the large sectional sofa, and the recently painted pool equipment shed.

Marian looked like she belonged with Kent. He was in his mid-forties, with deep green eyes, an athletic build, and thick brown hair that was graying near his temples. Marian was as glamorous as he was charming. She wore four-inch heels, form-fitting black slacks, and a lacy silk shirt that peeked out from under her suit jacket. Her shoulder-length, zero-frizz brown hair was several shades darker than mine.

Marian narrowed her eyes. "Kent didn't tell me about any upcoming redesign projects."

Say what? Kent had said Marian's birthday party was a surprise, but I couldn't believe he hadn't told her about the changes he was making.

Marian surveyed the backyard, then whipped her head toward me. "You broke into the shed?"

"Kent misplaced the key, so I bought a new lock before we popped off the old one," I explained as I slid off the float. Despite Kent's generous offer to use his pool, I suddenly felt like an unwelcome guest. It was clear Marian didn't want us in the pool on *her* floats. I hoped Erin would follow my lead and get off the pineapple.

"He didn't misplace the key," Marian said, then held up her set of keys. "I have it right here. The last time I flew to New York, Kent and his buddies went for a swim and popped two of my floats. This time I took the key with me." Marian scrunched up her face. "And please explain how you 'popped' off the lock. You didn't damage the shed, did you?"

I held up my hands as if surrendering. "No, I borrowed bolt cutters from my aunt." I had swung by her house this morning after buying a new lock and grabbing a coffee at Whisks and Whiskers, where I invited Erin to join me for an afternoon swim. "Aunt Deb owns the mini storage facility just south of Bonn Creek. She's the one who taught me how to use bolt cutters. You wouldn't believe how many times a week she has to use those suckers to cut through locks on sheds. Her tenants make a sport out of losing keys."

The incessant tapping of Marian's pointy-toed heel on the stone pavers made it clear she didn't care how many people lost their padlock keys. "Why is the shed yellow?" she demanded. "What was wrong with the red paint?"

I sighed. Kent had wanted Marian to be 'dazzled' by the redesign, but so far it appeared to be more of a fizzle. "I'm including yellow accents throughout the pool area because Kent said it's your favorite color," I explained.

Holding her dress up by its coat hanger, Marian shook it angrily. "Just because I own one yellow dress, he thinks it's my favorite color. Red is my favorite color, ladies. Red. I do not want this backyard drowning in yellow paint."

"It's nothing we can't change," I said. "I'll call the painter tonight and ask him to come out tomorrow and redo it. Would you like to go to the paint store with me to select the specific shade of red?"

"No. Leave it. I don't care anymore. I will change what I want when I have time, but I'm not bothering with this right now." She turned around and gazed at the empty cabana. "Where did all the furniture go?"

"Kent arranged for a Salvation Army truck to pick everything up two days ago," I said. "Don't worry, the new pieces are supposed to arrive soon."

"Who selected the new furniture? Kent? *You?*"

I nodded, seeing where this was going. There was a good

chance Marian would have wanted to help make selections. After all, it would soon be her backyard as well.

I pointed to pitcher on the side of the pool. "How about a strawberry-lemon mojito? I made them this afternoon. And I'd love to show you the furniture I've ordered. If there's anything you don't like, we can cancel the order and find something you'll be happy with." I was certain Kent wouldn't mind, now that Marian knew about the redesign.

Her face pinched as she squinted at me. "No, I don't want a mojito. Do you know how much sugar is in those things? And if you truly are Kent's new interior designer, please explain to me why you're in the pool right now instead of doing your job."

I understood she was upset Kent hadn't told her about the new furniture, but now she was being just plain condescending. I inhaled deeply through my nose, taking a moment to remind myself it was in my best interest to remain professional.

"Kent asked me to house sit—and dog sit—while he's away," I explained. "There are a lot of moving parts to a project like this and he wanted to make sure I was available to work around the clock." I gave myself a mental pat on the back for sounding far more patient that I felt. Yay for self-control.

"You're staying here?" Marian shrieked. "Tonight?"

"I've been here since Monday. Kent said I'm welcome to use the pool during downtime." He had told me to make myself at home and use anything—TV, entertainment system, kitchen appliances. He had even stocked his fridge with essentials he thought I would need. His house was essentially my house this week. "I assure you I'm working diligently on this project."

"Stop right there," Marian said. "I don't care what Kent said. I can see he and I are not aligned on appropriate boundaries for our work staff."

Erin signaled Marian with a wave. "Hey there, Marian. I'm Erin Blakely. My boyfriend, Rhett, works for Kent. I have heard *so* much about you. I've been hoping to meet you soon. Congrats on the engagement, by the way."

Erin's words were terse, her tone insincere. It was clear she was put off by Marian's rudeness.

Marian glared at us with folded arms, but Erin continued. "Anyway, Kent recently told my boyfriend he's looking to change things up back here, and *I'm* the one who recommended Hadley. Give her a chance."

Thankfully, Erin didn't mention she only met me five days ago.

Marian huffed. "Change things up, huh? Tell me, ladies, don't you think this is something I would like to help decide?"

"It's not too late," I reassured her again. "I can log onto my laptop right now and show you everything I've ordered."

"Don't bother. Finish your little project, and if I don't like it I'll hire my own designer and redo everything when I move in. I don't have time to mess with this right now. I just swung by to get my dress and take it to the dry cleaners, but I should probably burn it so Kent can get it through his head that yellow is not my favorite color. I want the two of you out of the pool and out of the house in ten minutes." Her eyes boomeranged between Erin and me as she spoke. "Get your stuff together and leave."

I returned my drink to the floating drink holder and paddled myself toward the pool stairs. "Come on," I whispered to Erin. "Time to go."

But she stayed on the pineapple, aiming a cold stare at Marian.

I turned back to Marian. "I don't want to stay here if it makes you uncomfortable, but someone needs to take care of Chip." At the mention of his name, Chip's howling intensified. "Kent told me Chip has difficulties staying away from home."

"I'm well aware of Chip's issues," she snapped. "I swear to you, when I move in, this dog is going to practically live at doggy daycare. He will have no choice but to get over his kennel anxiety. I refuse to be around this needy little rat all day."

Ouch. Poor Chip. I walked around the pool, picked him up, and held his shaking body against my chest. "Will you be able to stay here with Chip tonight since you're back in town early?"

Marian's lips parted, but she remained silent. She rattled the keys in her hand, as though reminding herself she had some place she had to be. A small keychain that looked like a dog dangled from her set of keys. How ironic, considering how much she seemed to dislike Chip.

Finally, Marian puffed her cheeks out and sighed. "I haven't moved in with Kent yet and I'm not taking the dog back to my house. You can stay here tonight and I will make other arrangements for Chip. Tomorrow night you will sleep at your own place. Understood?"

I nodded. "Or if it's easier, I can call Kent and ask if there's a neighbor who can—"

"No. Don't. He has an important business function tonight and I don't want you stressing him out." She turned abruptly and headed for the back door, clipping her heels against the smooth travertine pavers.

Chip continued fussing until Marian went inside the house and slammed the door. His body relaxed instantly in my arms.

I set him down. He pranced around the pool, wagging his tail and holding his head high. It was as though he were doing a victory lap after scaring Marian away with his ferocious barking.

CHAPTER TWO

"Hi, Kent, this is Hadley Sutton. Sorry to call during your business trip, but I wanted to talk to you about Chip. Marian came over this afternoon and we need to make other arrangements for him until you return. Also, we need to chat about some of the items I've ordered. Marian isn't too keen on yellow, so I need to make adjustments. Please call me when you get this. Thanks."

I ended the call, hoping my voicemail was compelling enough to prompt him to call me back. Shuffling across the carpet in Kent's upstairs guest room, I set my mobile phone on the nightstand. It was a little after ten o'clock and I was struggling to keep my eyes open.

Erin had left Kent's house in a huff this afternoon, still livid about how condescending Marian was. After watching her drive off in her black Honda, I paced Kent's kitchen, halls, and family room, staring at my phone while debating on whether to call him. I paused my pacing around eight o'clock to eat some leftover chicken and broccoli casserole I made earlier in the week. While I ate, I typed a dozen text messages to Kent but ended up deleting them before I hit send.

Marian had said Kent had an important work function and shouldn't be bothered, but he had instructed me to call anytime. I was certain he would want to know if Marian was going to relocate Chip, and I couldn't assume she would choose the ideal arrangements. Especially considering how she had spoken of Chip today.

For all I knew, she would drive him to another city, drop him off at the pound, and claim he had run away on my watch.

I also needed to talk to Kent about Marian's reaction to the redesign project. Obviously he wasn't as insightful about his fiancée's preferred color palette as he thought. Marian told me to not bother changing anything because she could hire her own designer if she didn't like my changes, but that would be a waste of Kent's money.

I wouldn't have felt so annoyed if I wasn't still reeling from getting dumped by my ex-boyfriend Ricky, while trying to create a backyard wonderland for an unappreciative woman whose fiancé wanted everything to be perfect for her. It took an extra dose of positive thinking and self-love to not feel jealous of Marian.

As rude and condescending as she had been, I wanted her to be pleased with the new outdoor living area. If I got the job at Walnut Ridge and moved to Darlington Hills, I hoped to use her as a reference for my Hadley Home Design business.

Most of my clients in New Orleans were referred to me by previous clients. Word-of-mouth recommendations were like free, turbo-charged advertisements. It would be devastating to my design business if Marian told everyone she had to redo all of my work.

Even though I had started my Hadley Home Design business after college and had enjoyed a slow but steady trickle of clients in New Orleans, it remained a side business for now. I still needed a full-time job to pay the bills.

That's why I applied for the interior design position at Walnut

Ridge Furniture and Decor in Darlington Hills. The owner was planning to issue his first-ever printed catalog and was hiring a designer to stage rooms with his furniture and accessories for catalog photoshoots.

The job was a long shot. I applied for it because I'd always loved coming to Darlington Hills to visit my aunt, uncle, and cousin when I was little. The town was a little slice of southern heaven. It had even been dubbed 'America's Friendliest City' by a southern travel journal. Aunt Deb loved to remind me of this fact.

Rummaging through my handbag, I located the sticky note on which Kent had written two phone numbers—his mobile number, which I had already saved in my phone, and the number for his hotel in Pennsylvania. Although I felt better after leaving a voicemail on his mobile phone, it was tempting to call his hotel. But I didn't want to bug him. At this late hour, it was possible he was already asleep.

The thought of sleep made me yawn. As much as I wanted to sit by the phone and wait for Kent to call, I needed to shower and go to bed. I'd have a busy day tomorrow canceling furniture orders and rethinking my design plans.

I set the sticky note on the nightstand next to my phone, then took a quick shower. After seeing how upset Marian was when I told her Kent asked me to house sit, I no longer felt comfortable sleeping here, much less taking a shower in his guest bathroom.

I wished I'd declined his request to house sit and stayed with Aunt Deb instead. That had been my original plan before I met Kent, and I'd been looking forward to spending time with her.

If I hadn't said yes to Kent, I'd probably be asleep in Aunt Deb's guest bed right now with my grandmother's quilt tucked under my chin. Years before she passed away, she made two quilts, one for each of her sons: my Uncle Bill—Aunt Deb's husband, who died on a fishing trip five years ago—and my Dad, who took his quilt with him when he and my mom relocated to a U.S. Air Force base in Japan before my freshman year in college.

After brushing my teeth and towel-drying my hair, I checked my phone again to see if Kent had returned my call.

No missed calls.

I turned out the lights, then slipped under the covers. Chip was already curled up at the foot of the bed, his chin resting on the comforter, looking up at me with big pouty eyes that were begging me to let him stay put.

"Good night, Chippy. If I let you sleep up here, you have to promise to be quiet." I leaned over and rubbed him behind his ears, then lay down and tried to think about anything besides Marian's condescending remarks and poor little Chip, who faced a bleak future of lonely kennels and a mean stepmother.

I awoke to the sound of a ringing phone somewhere in Kent's house, followed immediately by Chip's howling, which slit my ear drums and threw my heart into turbo speed.

"It's okay, Chip. It's just the phone." I rolled over, bringing one side of the pillow with me to cover my ear.

The phone rang again and Chip continued fussing. Abandoning my hopes for a quick return to sleep, I sat up and reached out to calm him. He jumped off the bed.

"Come on Chip, go back to sleep. Whoever it is can call back tomorrow." I patted the warm spot on the bed where he'd been laying.

Thanks to the street lamp in front of Kent's house and thin curtains, there was enough light in the room to see without needing to turn on the bedside lamp. Chip's body was stiff as he faced the closed door to the bedroom and continued to bark.

I lifted my phone from the nightstand and checked the time. Eight minutes after one o'clock. Who would call at this hour? I knew for certain they weren't trying to reach me. Anyone I knew would call my mobile phone. And if the caller knew Kent well enough, they would probably have his mobile number.

The phone stopped ringing and Chip settled down for all of five minutes until the phone rang again.

I tossed the covers aside and trudged toward the bedroom door. "Let's go tell whoever's calling to try back another time. Unless they want to come deal with a barking dog at one o'clock in the morning."

Stepping into the dark hallway, I headed for the stairs. It was logical Kent's landline phone would be in the kitchen or family room, even though I didn't recall seeing one.

The phone rang again and I stopped. It wasn't downstairs; it was somewhere up here, near me. Chip's barking made it difficult to pinpoint its exact location.

I reached down and picked him up, trying to calm him. Within a few seconds, his howls settled into a whimper. The ring came again and I turned toward its sound. The phone was in the room across from mine, which Kent had said was his office. I wanted to respect his privacy, but it would be a long night if I didn't answer the phone. "You think your daddy would mind if I went in there just for second?" I asked Chip, reaching for the door handle.

Rats. It was locked.

"Well, there goes that plan." Closing my eyes, I leaned my shoulder against the wall and waited for the ringing to stop, then padded back to the guest room and returned to bed. After several minutes of blissful silence, I relaxed enough to fall asleep.

Some time later, I awoke again. The phone was ringing again, but this time it was accompanied by a different sound—a series of thuds. I rubbed my eyes, trying to process what was going on. My phone told me it was just before 3:00 a.m.

Chip's ears perked up. He started growling, apparently too tired to bark. We both listened.

The thuds continued. I rubbed my eyes again. No, not thuds. Knocks. They were coming from downstairs.

This realization gave my cloudy mind the jolt it needed to wake up and think. Someone was at the front door. The phone was still ringing. Someone was trying to reach me.

I yanked my phone from the nightstand, ready to call the police if needed.

The knocks came again, louder this time. Chip howled and I bolted from the bed toward the window, which looked out on the front yard. Very slowly, I pulled the curtain aside and peeked out. There was a white SUV parked in Kent's driveway and a woman stood at the front door.

I rubbed the window to clear the spot my breath had fogged up. I squinted. Was the woman wearing a bathrobe?

The woman jerked her head up and looked directly at me. It wasn't Marian.

"Kent?" The woman's voice carried through the window. If she kept yelling, she was sure to wake the neighbors. "Please let me in."

With my phone still in-hand, I ran down the stairs and switched on the light in the entry way.

"Can I help you?" I asked, shouting through the front door.

"Marian?" The woman sounded confused.

"Marian isn't here right now. Who is this?"

"This is Celine, Marian's roommate. I'm worried about her. Can you let me in?"

If she was a thief and this was an elaborate ploy to get inside, she was quite skilled at her game. But she knew Marian's name, and she really did sound worried.

I cracked open the door. The woman was indeed in a robe, which partially covered a black pajama top. She had a shaggy blonde bob that was impressively stylish for three in the morning. "Why are you worried about Marian?"

"She hasn't come home yet and she isn't answering her phone. Is Kent home? He might know where she is."

I opened the door a little wider to study the woman: pink robe, lacy PJs, and Birkenstock sandals. Definitely not a thief. "Kent's in Philly and I don't know where Marian is." I took a step back and let Celine inside.

Without closing the door, Celine zipped past me toward the family room.

"Wait! Where are you going? You can't just—"

"Marian?" Celine yelled. She circled around the sofa and end table, then headed for Kent's room. "Marian?"

I followed Celine, and Chip stayed close to me. He barked incessantly, his head jerking up and down so violently I worried it would give him whiplash.

"I told you, Marian isn't here," I repeated as I picked up Chip. "Neither is Kent, which is why I'm house sitting this week while I work on his outdoor living area. I'm an interior designer."

Celine stopped in the arched opening between Kent's bedroom and bathroom, flipped on a light and looked around, then fixed her dark brown eyes on me. "An interior designer who house sits? Yeah, right. And don't tell me this is none of my business. Marian has a right to know Kent is cheating on her."

"He's not cheating. Kent is my client," I said, practically hollering to talk over the barking. "Kent is throwing a surprise birthday party for Marian next week and he—"

"I know about the surprise party," she snapped. "Kent asked me to be in charge of the guest list."

I closed my eyes and sighed, seriously regretting my decision to let her in the house. "Anyway, he hired me less than a week ago to redo his patio area because he wants everything to be perfect for Marian. And he needed someone to care for Chip since he doesn't like to leave the house. I explained all of this to Marian when she came over yesterday afternoon. Well, except for the part about the surprise party. She wasn't happy about me staying here—understandably—and we both agreed I will leave the house tomorrow when I finish working."

Celine pulled back her chin. "Marian came over here yesterday? And you spoke with her?"

"Yes, around five o'clock. She seemed like she was in a hurry to leave."

She gave a curt nod. "Probably so she could call Kent and yell at him for inviting another woman to stay at his house. That must be why she was in such a huff when she came home in the evening. She only stayed for five minutes and then left. She hasn't come home yet and I can't reach her on her phone."

Chip stopped barking, which gave me more brainpower to think. Why was Celine so worried about Marian? Did she always keep track of her roommate's whereabouts? Marian was a grown woman.

I flipped off the light to the bathroom and moved toward the bedroom door, hoping Celine would follow me. This was Kent's private space. I didn't feel right being in there, but I couldn't help but glance around at his bedroom decor. The style was traditional, just like the rest of his home. The deep-brown mahogany chest of drawers near the door matched his mirrored dresser and four-post bed. His walls were a light olive green, which complemented the rich red tones of the furniture. The bedspread was neutral—a light gray linen duvet with deeper gray pillow shams. Two white decorative pillows sat on either side of round pillow featuring a cross-stitched kangaroo.

Celine followed me out of Kent's room and back to the entry hall. Marian's friend or not, she didn't need to be snooping around Kent's house.

"Do you have the phone app that lets you find your friends?" I asked. My ever-cautious roommate in college had insisted we share each other's locations for safety reasons.

Celine grunted. "Don't you think I would have tried that if I could? Marian uses her work phone and her company disabled that functionality, along with a slew of other useful features."

Good grief. Celine was as condescending as Marian. I folded my arms and leaned against the front door, ready to bid this woman goodbye.

"Maybe Marian had to leave town again and forgot to tell you?" I suggested.

Celine shook her head. "No. She walked to the town square to run errands. Her car's still in the driveway."

My eyes widened. That was odd. No wonder Celine was worried.

"Maybe she took a cab somewhere?" I said.

She slumped forward, like a balloon that was slowly deflating. "She hates cabs. Marian would walk five miles in the rain before she stepped inside a cab."

"Has she ever done anything like this before? Stayed out all night without her car?"

"No, except for when she's with Kent."

I rubbed my eyes, wishing I could be more helpful. But three o'clock in the morning wasn't my prime time for brilliant ideas. "You said she was in a huff when she came home? Did she say why?"

"She and I aren't really..." Celine trailed off, her gaze shifting to the door. "I don't know what was wrong, but I could tell something was off."

"Have you called the police?" I asked.

She whipped her eyes back to me. "You think I should? I've been telling myself I'm overreacting, that there's a logical explanation for this. I was hoping I'd be able to reach her, or maybe Kent would know where she is."

I nodded. "I'd call them. She hasn't been gone long, but it sounds like this is a big change in her normal routine." I didn't want to be an alarmist, but it was odd that Marian hadn't returned from her evening errands. I was a little surprised Celine hadn't called the cops already.

Celine yanked her robe tight across her chest and moved toward the door. "I'll go by the police station on my way home," she muttered. "Fill out a missing persons report or whatever."

We exchanged phone numbers and I gave her the number to Kent's hotel room in Philly.

"I'm sorry," I said. "I know how worried you are. If I hear anything about Marian, I'll be sure to call you." I held the door open, giving her a reassuring smile as she walked out. "Try not to worry, sweetie. I'm sure Marian is fine."

She turned two watery, bloodshot eyes at me. "This is your fault, you know. I don't believe your 'I have to take care of Kent's dog' excuse, and I am certain Marian didn't either. I can't even imagine what she's gone and done because of you."

CHAPTER THREE

"Tell me where you'd like it, ma'am." Paul from Paul's Lighting and Such pulled a large, black cast-aluminum wall lantern out of its box. He kicked the box aside with his work boot and carefully set down the light fixture on the patio.

I walked to the stone fireplace on the far side of the cabana and stood on the elevated seating ledge. "Right here, centered on the wall above the fireplace. The lantern should be even with the top of the pergolas." I motioned to the structures on either side of the fireplace.

"You got it." Paul popped open a rusty red toolbox and retrieved a level, tape measure, and stick of chalk. "Your client's gonna like this lantern. It's one of my personal favorites. All the trendy folks are buying it these days. Good choice, ma'am."

I smiled. "Thanks." I wasn't feeling as chatty as Paul. It was 7:30 a.m. and I was running on less than four hours of sleep and zero caffeine. After Celine left, it took me two hours to fall asleep. I slept through my alarm—or perhaps turned it off in a near-dead stupor of sleep—and awoke to the sound of Paul knocking on the front door.

Now, I was regretting my decision to schedule the installation of the light fixtures so early in the morning. I'd even paid extra for this time slot since it was outside of Paul's normal business hours. But it had to get done this week to meet Kent's timeline, and all the regular-hour time slots were booked for the next two weeks.

Opening his A-frame ladder, Paul gave me a quick once-over. "I thought I knew all the interior designers in Darlington Hills. There's only a few of them. You must be new to town?"

"I don't live here; I'm from New Orleans. Just visiting this week." I would save all the details of that particular story for a day when I wasn't a walking zombie.

Paul laughed. "So you're the one who brought the sunny weather to town. Early March hasn't been this warm in ages. And I speak the truth when I say that. I've lived here my entire life."

"You must have known my dad and uncle, Brady and Bill Sutton," I said. Paul looked to be in his early sixties, so it was likely he went to school with them.

Paul gave another hearty chuckle as he climbed the ladder. "The Sutton boys. You bet I knew them. I got into my fair share of trouble with those two when I was younger." He placed the level and stick of chalk on the top rung of the ladder, then studied my face. "That explains why you look so familiar."

Possibly. Or, most likely, it was because I had a familiar face. Apparently there were a lot of women with brown eyes and wavy light-brown hair in their early thirties who looked like me. The only thing that set me apart from all my lookalikes was the scar above my right eyebrow that I earned during my first interior design attempt. I was rearranging furniture in my bedroom and a lamp fell off my chest-of-drawers and hit me. I was nine when it happened.

"How's your dad doing these days?" Paul asked.

"He's still in Tokyo with my mom, but he's planning to retire in a couple of years."

"Last I saw him was at his brother's funeral, God rest Bill's

soul. I never did understand what happened on his boat that day."
He shook his head sadly.

"They say he fell off and hit his head on the side of the boat on
his way into the water," I said. The police had investigated, but
closed the case after a couple of weeks, saying it was an accident.

Stretching the tape measure across the width of the stone wall
of the fireplace, he shook his head. "None of us believe that
explanation. Not one word of it."

Paul reminisced about his childhood and all the fun he had
with my dad and uncle. I caught bits and pieces of his stories
about their days on the baseball field, but my thoughts kept
drifting to the four words that had kept me awake after Celine
left: 'this is your fault.'

If Marian was still missing, did her disappearance have
anything to do with me? Had she seen me in Kent's pool and
assumed her fiancé was cheating on her? Had she gotten cold feet
before her wedding and run? I wished I had told Marian the
truth, that I was there because Kent wanted everything done
perfectly and in time for her birthday party. So what if I would
have ruined a surprise?

It was alarming that Marian hadn't returned after her errands.
If she had run, it seemed like she would have taken her car or at
least a suitcase. I doubted foul play was involved because
Darlington Hills was a safe town, so said Aunt Deb and Trip-
Advisor.

Of course, all of my worrying could be pointless if Marian
had walked through her front door this morning. I had texted
Celine first thing today, between racing to get dressed and flying
down the stairs to greet Paul, but she hadn't returned my text. I
couldn't decide if that was a good sign or bad one.

Paul left at 8:15 a.m., leaving me forty-five minutes to feed
Chip, inhale some coffee, eat breakfast, and shove all of my stuff
into my suitcase before SunChic Furniture was scheduled to
deliver the outdoor sectional. Another company was supposed to

deliver the tables and lounge chairs for the pool deck between two and four o'clock, and then I could call a cab and head over to Aunt Deb's house.

If I'd had my car with me in Virginia, I'd have stored my suitcase in the trunk because I would be one step closer to leaving.

After I rounded up all my stuff and put the guest bed sheets in the washing machine, I sat at the kitchen table with my binder for Kent's outdoor redesign project. Over the years, I had collected dozens of one-inch, three-ring binders for all my clients' projects.

I flipped to the vendor tab and found the company from which I'd ordered the yellow patio umbrellas and decorative pillows. I dialed the number, then took a sip of coffee. A lady answered after the first ring.

"Hello!" I said, rushing to swallow my sip. "This is Hadley Sutton. I placed an order on Tuesday and I need to change the color of—"

My phone beeped, signaling another call. I glanced at the caller ID: Philadelphia West Regent Hotel.

"Sorry, I'll have to call back later." I switched to the other call. "Hello?"

"Hey there, Hadley," Kent said. "Good morning. I saw you called me yesterday and I'm sorry I didn't pick up. I'm embarrassed to admit it but I got a little too carried away with the gin and tonics last night at the gala we sponsored and I had to end my evening early—and rather ungracefully, I might add." He let out a low chuckle. "I haven't had a night like that since college."

Though Kent's voice was deep and gravely, he sounded upbeat. I relaxed a little, thinking that was a good sign everything was fine with Marian. He'd probably spoken with her earlier this morning.

"I listened to your voicemail, and I understand you met Marian yesterday. If she doesn't want yellow umbrellas, I'm fine with changing the colors to whatever she prefers. And by the way, I didn't realize she was coming home early. I would have given you a heads-up had I known."

"No, it's fine. Really." His fiancée, on the other hand, was not so fine with everything.

"You didn't mention the surprise party to her, right?" His tone was light, as though he were asking me if I'd remembered to turn the lights off in a room. But I knew how important it was to keep the party a surprise.

"Nope, not a word," I replied. "But have you spoken with her—"

"Okay, good. I want her party to be the surprise of all surprises." Another phone rang in the background, likely his mobile phone. The ringing grew louder and then stopped abruptly. "I need to get going soon, but do you need anything else from me? Is everything else on track for the patio?"

"Yes, but have you—"

"Wonderful. Then please change any colors necessary and carry on with your plans. I love everything you showed me and if we need to do some tweaking later on, I'll be sure to let you know." He laughed. "Just make sure you move to Darlington Hills, okay?"

"Yes, I hope to. And one more thing before you go, have you talked to Marian this morning?"

"Not yet. I texted her when I woke up but haven't heard from her." There was a pause. "Why?"

My heart picked up its pace. "Have you talked to Celine today?"

"You know Celine? You don't waste time making friends in a new town, do you?" He chuckled again. "Celine called several times last night. I put her in charge of the guest list for Marian's party and she's taking her job quite seriously."

"She came over early this morning and said Marian didn't come home last night," I said, speaking as fast as I could so he wouldn't interrupt me again. I couldn't imagine conversations between him and Marian getting anywhere considering how much the two of them cut people off. "She was really worried, Kent. She said she called and texted Marian repeatedly, but couldn't reach her."

"When did Celine see her last?" His gravelly voice was now filled with concern.

"Apparently Marian left her house to run errands yesterday afternoon around five, and never returned home. Her car is still in her driveway."

"Something's not right. Marian always answers her phone." He paused for a moment, and there was a tapping on the other side, like nervous fingers repeatedly hitting a table. "She has family about an hour away who she visits occasionally but she always drives there. Hang on a second; I'm going to check my phone."

Not good. He hadn't heard from Marian and he didn't have any logical explanations for where she could have gone. I stood and paced around the kitchen.

"She didn't call me last night," he said, alarm overtaking his cheery tone. "Marian always calls me before she goes to sleep. Did she seem okay yesterday when she came over? She may have had another disagreement with Celine."

"Marian was angry yesterday, but I think it had something to do with finding Erin and me swimming in your pool." I swallowed hard as Celine's words flashed through my mind: *This is all your fault.*

"Ah, yes. I can see how that might upset her. Did she seem to believe your excuse?"

I frowned. Believe my excuse? It wasn't an excuse; it was the truth.

"I explained who I am and why I'm staying at your house this week. Even so, Marian did not feel comfortable with the situation, so I told her I was happy to leave if arrangements were made for Chip."

"Okay, I'll try to reach her at the office, and if needed I'll call her coworkers and see if they've heard from her. If I don't hear from her, I'll fly home today. I'm also going to call the police and have them start a search."

"Celine said she would go to the police this morning when she left your house," I said.

He grunted. "I'm calling them anyway. Celine doesn't always do what she says she's going to do. Hang tight, please stay with Chip, and I'll keep you updated on Marian."

CHAPTER FOUR

I slid the patio chair to the right, then to the left, then forward. There. Perfect.

I shook my head. No, not perfect. Too close to the coffee table. Too far from the sectional.

Kicking off my flip flops, I sank into the plush cushion of Kent's brand new outdoor sectional sofa. The upholstery was stretched tight and even from one side of the sofa to the other, and the woven fabric was soft against my legs.

A crew from SunChic Furniture had delivered it earlier this morning along with swivel chairs, ottomans, end tables, and two coffee tables. All of the furniture in the cabana was made of bronze cast-aluminum and had chestnut-colored seat cushions.

It was two o'clock in the afternoon, and I'd been rearranging the furniture for the past several hours. I had to keep my body moving to prevent my mind from racing. Neither Kent nor Celine had called or texted, so all I could do was worry.

A man from the final delivery crew of the day came through the gate and into the backyard, holding a chaise lounge. "Where do you want this one, miss?"

I stood. "I'd like it by the other one over there." I pointed to the left side of the pool deck, where another delivery man was positioning the matching chaise lounge. "There will be four groups of two—one pair by each corner of the pool."

I thanked him and continued arranging the furniture in the cabana. The space was taking shape, but it still felt empty without the area rug, throw pillows and other items I had ordered, which were scheduled to arrive tomorrow and Sunday. I always told clients the furniture is like the cake and all the other decor was the icing.

And a cake isn't a cake without heaps of icing.

The afternoon was warm like yesterday, but today there was a steady breeze that carried a chill, as though Mother Nature was reminding us summer was still months away. It was ideal weather for sitting outside with a book and blanket and listening to all the happy sounds of early spring.

But while the birds busied themselves chirping, I worked diligently on Kent's cabana. Everything had to be perfect, even if Marian would want to make changes later.

The delivery crew finished, and I signed their form to confirm everything had arrived in good condition. Two minutes after they left, the front doorbell chimed.

I ran inside the house toward the door. Chip scurried alongside me, his howl echoing in the marble-tiled entryway. "Coming!" I yelled.

Hopefully it was Celine—or better yet, Marian. Maybe she was here with fabric samples and paint swatches, ready to redesign her soon-to-be backyard paradise.

I swooped Chip into my arms, and without looking through the peephole, flung open the door.

A police office held up his badge. "Afternoon, Miss. I'm Officer Dennis Appley with the Darlington Hills Police Department. Are you Hadley?"

My heart thudded double-time as I imagined all the reasons he might be on Kent's doorstep. None of them were good. "Yes, Hadley Sutton. Nice to meet you. Is this about Marian?"

"Yes, ma'am." The officer's tone was serious, but his blue eyes carried hints of a smile, as though he didn't let his job interfere too much with his sense of humor. He looked young, maybe mid- to late twenties, and with his tousled sandy blonde hair, he looked more like a college frat guy than a police officer. "What do you know about Ms. Marian Koh?"

"I know she's missing," I blurted out. "Or, at least that's what her roommate told me when she came over here at three o'clock this morning. Has she been found? Probably not, since you're here asking about her."

Words were flying out of my mouth faster than I could think about whether I was making sense.

I took a deep breath, then continued. "I met Marian for the first time yesterday. She came over here around five in the afternoon, stayed for less than ten minutes, and then left. Then her roommate, Celine, came over early this morning and told me Marian went to run errands yesterday evening and never returned home."

Officer Appley fixed his eyes on me as I spoke. "Yes, Celine reported her roommate's disappearance this morning. She suggested we send someone over here to look around."

My jaw dropped. What had Celine told the police? That they should come ask me questions because it was my fault Marian went missing?

"What is the extent of your relationship with Kent Reading?" he asked.

I flinched. "Relationship? He and I are not in a relationship." Had Celine told the police Kent and I were romantically involved? "I've only known him for five days. I flew in last weekend for a job interview. The interview was postponed, but I snagged this small client project to occupy my time while I'm here. I'm redesigning his outdoor living space."

"So it's a business relationship?" The officer did a quick head-to-toe scan, making me regret wearing the shortest pair of shorts in my suitcase today.

"Yes, it is strictly professional."

Officer Appley raised an eyebrow. "I've been told you're staying at Mr. Reading's house this week. Is that part of your interior design package?"

I rolled my eyes. Clearly, Celine told the police she thought I was more than just Kent's designer. "No, officer. I do not typically house sit when I'm working on a client project." I shifted Chip to my other arm while I explained the short timeline and Marian's upcoming birthday party. "Kent wanted to make sure everything was finished in one week since I fly home to New Orleans on Monday."

He nodded, but it seemed more like an I-hear-what-you're-saying nod than an I-believe-you nod. "Tell me about your conversation with Ms. Koh yesterday."

"She came home early from a business trip and was surprised to find me in her fiancé's backyard. Kent hadn't told her he hired me because he wanted to keep the redesign a surprise. It was clear she didn't want me staying at the house, so I promised I would leave as soon as someone made other arrangements for his dog."

"What were you doing when Marian came over?" he asked.

I gulped. "Taking a break."

"Where, specifically?"

"In the pool. On a float."

Officer Appley's eyebrows climbed higher. "Do you make use of all your clients' amenities? Or is that privilege unique to your 'strictly professional' relationship with Mr. Reading?"

I tossed up my hands. "I am not in a relationship with Kent. Want to know why? Because I met him five days ago. Because I don't date clients. And, most importantly, I am taking a break from men right now because my heart and ego are on the injured reserve list thanks to Ricky, my egocentric ex-boyfriend back in New Orleans, who left me three weeks ago because he's more in love with his career as a morning TV news anchor than me."

The subtle smile in Officer Appley's eyes spread to his face, making his cheek dimple. He held up his palms. "Okay, okay. I get it. Your relationship…I mean, your association with Mr. Reading is entirely professional. Poolside breaks and all."

My cheeks burned. Even the slightest mention of Ricky fired me up. I was interviewing for the job in Darlington Hills so I could move far, far away from every life-size cardboard cutout of Ricky that advertised his morning news show and encouraged New Orleanians to 'spend the morning with Ricky Countryman.'

"Did Ms. Koh say anything else to you that may be of importance?" he asked.

"No," I said, then paused a moment to clear my head of Ricky and focus on the officer's question. "Marian looked like she'd come from a business meeting," I recalled. "She was in a pantsuit with heels—nice ones that looked really expensive—and she had a yellow dress slung over her arm. She said she had stopped by to pick it up and take it to the dry cleaners. I don't know how many dry cleaners there are in town, but maybe you could check with them."

He nodded. "Thanks for the tip."

"Have you gotten in touch with Kent yet?" I asked. "I spoke with him earlier today and he said he would fly back if he wasn't able to reach Marian."

"We talked to him. He's coming home this afternoon." Officer Appley stretched his neck to the side, looking inside Kent's house through the open door.

"Want to come inside, have a look around?" Taking a step back, I opened the door wider. I couldn't imagine him finding anything that would be helpful, but I figured he would want to try. "Kent won't mind; I know he wants you guys to do everything you can to find her."

Stepping inside, Officer Appley dipped his head as though to thank me. "You're the designated house sitter, so I'll take you up on that offer." He motioned toward the wood-paneled office to the left of the entry hall. "After you, miss. You're the tour guide."

I showed him around downstairs, then outside in the backyard. By the time we headed upstairs, Chip had calmed down and was trotting cheerfully behind Officer Appley. I took him into the guest bedroom, emphasizing it was the room I had been sleeping in. Just in case he still had any doubts about my relationship with Kent.

We stepped briefly inside the second bedroom upstairs, which had been converted into a home gym with mirrors on one wall, several racks with weights on another, and interlocking rubber tiles covering the floor. This was an amenity I had not made use of during my stay at Kent's.

Out in the hallway again, I headed back toward the stairs. Officer Appley pointed to the third door in the hallway.

"What's in this room?" he asked, pressing on the door handle as he walked by.

"It's Kent's office."

He frowned. "I thought the room downstairs with all the wood was the office. He has two?"

I shrugged. "He called the one downstairs his study and this one the office."

"Sounds like the same thing to me. Have you gone in there?"

"I tried to last night when the phone wouldn't stop ringing, but it was locked."

Officer Appley studied the door, then stood on his tiptoes and ran his hand along the top of the doorframe.

My eyes widened. He was looking for a key.

His arm fell to his side. "I sure would like to take a peek in this room."

"You think she's in there?" I whispered. Goosebumps pricked

my neck as I considered the possibility that Marian was in the locked room while I slept across the hall last night.

"No. Based on information you and Celine provided, it sounds like Marian left this house at five o'clock, drove home, and then left on foot to run errands." Officer Appley took a step back from the door, continuing to sweep his eyes across it. "You sure you don't have a key to this door? Seems like it would be part of the house-sitting gig."

I stifled a laugh. "No, he didn't give me a key to this room."

"Well, I can't open this lock without a warrant, but if you happen to be in need of something like a pair of scissors or stapler, you'd be able to open it with a simple hairpin." His eyes opened a little wider, as though he were hoping I would need some office supplies at that exact moment.

"Is that an invitation to break the law, officer?"

"As long as you don't take anything, I'd say a quick visit inside this room would be well within your official duties as the house sitter."

Taking a step closer to him, I narrowed my eyes at the stunning sea-blue ones staring back at me. I was certain he had a habit of getting whatever he wanted with those eyes. "I don't use hairpins, I don't need to staple anything, and I absolutely do not feel comfortable intruding into Kent's locked room." I turned and walked down the stairs, then opened the front door for Officer Appley.

After writing down my phone number, he stepped outside, then reached in the front pocket of his police uniform and pulled out a card. "Here's my number. Call if you have any more information to share about Marian Koh, or if you happen to look inside the office upstairs."

I plucked the card from his hand. "I will not 'happen to look' in his office, thank you very much. I take my house-sitting duties seriously."

His cheek dimpled. "Your professionalism is commendable. Thanks for the tour, Miss Hadley."

Miss Hadley? My heart swiftly flip-flopped, something it hadn't done since I'd first met my ex-boyfriend. As I watched Officer Appley stroll to his patrol car, a smile crawled across my face.

If I moved to Darlington Hills, there was a distinct possibility my self-imposed dating hiatus wouldn't last very long.

CHAPTER FIVE

"Your daddy will be home soon," I reassured Chip as I straightened the family room. His ears perked up at the sound of his name, and his tail started wagging furiously.

I had kept Kent's house clean and tidy, but I needed something to do to keep me busy until Kent arrived. Officer Appley had told me his flight was supposed to arrive later this afternoon.

In the two hours since Officer Appley left, I arranged the furniture that was delivered earlier, put clean sheets on the guest bed, cleaned the bathroom, and vacuumed every room in the house. Worry had turned me into a domestic enthusiast.

I fluffed two more decorative couch pillows, then ventured into the kitchen to look for something else to clean. My options were limited, as every surface of every appliance gleamed as though it were straight out of the box.

After one more pass of the vacuum around the breakfast table, I decided to cook dinner for Kent. He probably wouldn't take the time to eat on his way home from the airport, and I wanted to try out the fancy three-in-one electric cooking machine on his counter. It was about the size of a microwave, with a miniature pull handle on the front that opened to a small oven. On the top was a frying pan, and a partitioned egg boiler. The machine was glossy red with chrome accents, reminding me of a high-end sports car or motorcycle.

Pulling open the refrigerator and freezer, I inventoried my options for dinner: half a carton of eggs, four pieces of frozen chicken, and a slew of vegetables that looked every bit as fresh as they had four days ago, thanks to Kent's fridge and its super-engineered 'Stay Fresh' technology.

"I hope your daddy is hungry when he gets home," I said, pulling the vegetable tray from the fridge. Chip looked up at me expectantly. "Don't worry, sweetie. It's almost your dinner time too."

Ten minutes later the machine dinged, telling me it was preheated. I crammed four chicken breasts on the aluminum tray and closed the door. According to the instruction manual, the frozen chicken needed to bake for fifty minutes on the medium-high setting. I would need to wait a little while to start the eggs and veggies since they wouldn't take as long to cook.

I walked to the pantry and retrieved a can of dog food from the shelf. Chip ran micro-circles around the table leg, barking at me to hurry up and put his food in his bowl.

"Hang on buddy," I laughed. "I have to open it first."

My phone rang and I nearly dropped the can of dog food. I held up a finger at Chip. "Sorry, I need to get this first." I jogged over to the kitchen table and grabbed my phone.

The words Philadelphia West Regent Hotel flashed on my screen. Kent? Was he still in Pennsylvania? Hope swelled through my heart. Maybe he had stayed because he reached Marian.

"Hello?" I said.

No one responded, but there was a long, heavy sigh on the other end of the phone.

"Kent?"

"Hi, Hadley. I'm coming home today, but I won't arrive until a little after three a.m. There was a multi-car pileup and traffic jam on my way to the airport earlier this afternoon and I missed my flight."

I didn't need to ask Kent if he'd heard from Marian. His voice was so shaky I knew he was holding back tears.

"Would you mind staying there one more night with Chip?" he asked.

I cringed. The last thing I wanted was to stay another night as his place. I'd been looking forward to a night without angry roommates stopping by or continuous phone calls in the middle of the night.

"Of course," I said, throwing Chip a weak smile. As much as I didn't want to stay, I wouldn't leave Chip by himself.

"Thanks, Hadley. I can't tell you how much that means to me at a time like this. I'd like you to keep working on the backyard. I'm going to text Marian photos of it when you're finished. Maybe that will change her mind."

Wherever Marian was, I doubted photos of the backyard decor that she didn't have any input on would convince her of Kent's love. But, a job was a job and I would see it through to the end.

"Sure, I understand," I said. "Everything will be done by Sunday. We just have a few more deliveries this weekend, and the painter needs to redo the equipment shed. Marian prefers red."

"Oh, um, actually I'd like to keep the shed yellow. I couldn't stand the red paint; it reminded me of a barn."

I pulled the phone away and stared at it. He didn't want to give in to his missing fiancée's preference for the paint color? I no longer had any doubt that if Marian returned, she would redo all my work, beginning with the shed.

"Oh, Hadley! I'm so sorry to hear Marian is missing!" Aunt Deb jogged up Kent's sidewalk, her frilly skirt swirling around her ankles. She held out her arms, enveloping me in a hug of soft cashmere and love.

"Thanks for coming over. Staying by myself while waiting for news on Marian is making me go crazy. I've vacuumed four times this afternoon."

She smiled. "You get that from your daddy. Your mother always told me her house was never cleaner than when something was on his mind."

I pulled back my chin. "That's why Dad vacuums so much? I always assumed he was just helping out around the house."

"I'm sure that's his side of the story, but it's a nervous habit of his. Just ask your mom, she'll tell you. I always lamented the fact your dear Uncle Bill didn't inherit that compulsive trait. It would've put all his fussing to good use."

Aunt Deb removed her car key from her purse and held it up, pressing one of the buttons. Her car responded with a single beep and flash of the front headlights. The street was quiet, with the only light coming from the dim lamp posts in front of each house.

"Do you know Marian well?" I asked.

Aunt Deb seemed to know everyone in Darlington Hills. She had lived here for the past thirty years, ever since she married my uncle when she was twenty-five. They raised their son, Michael, in a two-story home attached to the leasing office of the business they owned and operated, Darlington Mini Storage. But now that Michael lived in Chicago and Uncle Bill had passed, Aunt Deb ran the facility by herself.

"I know of Marian, but I haven't met her," Aunt Deb said. "She moved here a few months ago and she's always traveling. But my friend Patty has a daughter who colors Marian's hair at Snippets Salon. From what Patty tells me, Marian is as snooty as they come. Nevertheless, I hope the poor dear is okay. I can't imagine why she would've run off."

I winced, recalling Celine's harsh accusation that it was my fault. I told Aunt Deb about Marian finding Erin and me floating in Kent's pool, and how angry she was when I told her I was staying the week at his house. "I wish I had told her about the surprise party. Ruining the surprise would have been better than her thinking I was more than Kent's interior designer."

Aunt Deb shook her head, her thick auburn hair swishing around her shoulders. "This isn't your fault, hon. Even if Marian has issues with jealousy, her running off has nothing to do with you."

I wasn't so sure. "If she doesn't return before tomorrow, then I'll look for her myself." I'd form a search party, put up fliers, and help make phone calls.

"I'm sure the police can use all the help they can get," she said. "Just don't do it out of guilt."

Somewhere across the street, wind chimes sounded. Moments later the shrubs in Kent's yard shook furiously from gusts of an approaching cold front.

I folded my arms across my chest. "I should have stuck to my original plan and stayed with you this week. Then we could have chit-chatted for hours on end. I wish we could have done more of that this week."

She waved her hand dismissively. "I don't wanna hear any should-ofs or could-ofs. You'll just have to get the job at that furniture company, move here, and settle down. You can find a nice man—there are plenty in Darlington Hills—and get married and—oh! There's a lovely wedding dress store two blocks south of the town square."

I stared at her, my mouth open.

"We could stop by tomorrow morning after your interview. I know you and Ricky just broke up, but it's never too early to start looking. For dresses or for men."

"Um, no." I turned my feet toward the house.

"Hmm. Well then maybe we should start by finding you a place to live. I'd like to show you a couple of popular apartment complexes in town. They're both a five-minute walk from my place, so you and I would practically be neighbors."

I smiled at the thought of having my own place in Darlington Hills. Growing up, my mom, dad, and I came here every Christmas and sometimes during the summer. It was one of my favorite places on earth, with its friendly southern charm and cozy, tree-lined streets. Now, depending on how my interview went tomorrow, there was a chance I could call this town my own.

"Let's see how the interview goes, and then maybe we can go apartment hunting. I don't want to jinx anything." I rubbed my bare arms as another rush of wind whistled by us, then gestured toward the front door. "Are you hungry? I hope you like Asian food. Before Kent told me he missed his flight, I started making him honey garlic chicken and stir fry veggies for dinner. But now it's ours to enjoy."

She hiked up her skirt as she climbed the porch steps. "I'm starvin', darlin'. Let's eat."

I opened the door and we stepped inside. My hand flew to my nose.

"There's a natural gas leak!" Aunt Deb shouted.

"The eggs!" I cried.

Chip joined the hollering hoopla with his own ferocious yapping.

I ran through the foul, gaseous cloud into the kitchen toward the source of the stench—the electric dinner machine. The plastic dome above the automatic egg boiler was cloudy, making me hesitate to release more of the swirling steam into the house.

Grabbing a pair of tongs and holding my breath, I threw back the dome, plucked the eggs from the now-scorched aluminum tray, and threw them into the trash. It smelled like I'd set off a stink bomb in Kent's house.

Aunt Deb raced around the kitchen and breakfast nook, opening windows while I took the trash bag out to the garbage can in the garage. When I returned, Chip was still going crazy, his high-pitch shrieks echoing throughout the house. Aunt Deb had her hand in a box of Kent's cereal.

She tossed a sugary puff to Chip. "Here you go, sweetie. You don't need to bark at me. I'm here to spoil you, just like I used to spoil Hadley when she was a little girl."

Chip stopped barking. He sat on his haunches, looked up at Aunt Deb, and wagged his tail.

"That isn't on his diet," I told her. "Kent specifically said no table food."

Aunt Deb swished a hand at me and gave Chip several more pieces. "This isn't from the table. It's from a box." She squatted down, opened her arms, and picked him up when he came running. "See there, he just needs some variety in his diet. He's tired of whatever mush comes from that can over there."

Aunt Deb shifted her gaze to Kent's dinner machine. "What *is* that thing?"

"It's a three-in-one electric cooker. It has a mini frying pan, oven, and automatic egg cooker—which appears to have some flaws." I hustled to the machine and removed the veggies, which had fortunately survived. The chicken had another fifteen minutes to go.

Aunt Deb looked around the kitchen, her brow furrowing. "Is there something wrong with the stove and oven?"

"No, I just wanted to try out the multi-cooker in case I can afford one someday. Imagine the possibilities—cooking an entire meal using only one appliance!"

Aunt Deb hovered over the machine. "I don't think I want to imagine that scenario. And Hadley, hon, if you're going to burn eggs, you might as well burn them on the stove." She pulled on the machine's tiny oven handle. "This looks like an adult version of an Easy Bake oven. You know, like the one you got for Christmas when you were seven or eight. Remember? And come to think of it, I think you burnt the cookies you made with that toy as well."

"This machine isn't a toy," I said, laughing. "I just need to figure out the issue with the eggs." I picked up the machine's thick instruction manual and turned to the section on the egg cooker. "See, it says right here that it cooks up to five eggs to perfection in no time."

She scrunched her nose. "They have an unusual definition of perfection, don't they?"

I shrugged. "Oh well. So much for the deviled eggs. We'll have to come up with another side dish."

Aunt Deb straighten her back. "Deviled eggs?"

"Yes, there were half a dozen eggs left in the fridge and Kent had most of the required ingredients. I figured it would be something nice for him."

She seemed to consider this. "I can't say I've made deviled eggs for any occasion besides Easter brunch, and definitely not alongside an Asian stir fry dish. The culinary choices of your generation never cease to astound me."

"Haven't you heard of fusion dishes?" I asked, playfully mimicking her disdain.

"It's more like *con*fusion."

"Think of fusion as a creative intermingling of different cultures, traditions, tastes, and textures. It's my generation's collective response to a childhood of Hamburger Helper and frozen pizza."

Aunt Deb whistled. "I'm telling your mama you said that. Hamburger Helper is her specialty."

After the chicken was finished, we ate at the table in the breakfast nook and enjoyed Kent's dinner while Chip sat in Aunt Deb's lap and enjoyed the many pieces that 'fell' from her fork.

At half past nine, Aunt Deb walked out to her car and drove home. With Chip by my side, I lay down on the sofa in the family room, wishing more than anything I was in the car with her.

CHAPTER SIX

I awoke to the sound of a window opening—the screech of a dirty frame sliding against a dirty window track, accompanied by a grunt.

I flew off the couch. Someone was in the dark corner by the window. On *my* side of the window.

The person moved toward me and I bolted for the front door.

A strong hand grasped my upper arm and spun me around. "Marian?"

"Let go!" I yelled, kicking the man in the shin.

"Who are you?" he demanded, still holding my arm. Then, in the same breath, "Is Kent here?"

"I'm Hadley. I'm house sitting." Immediately, I regretted giving the intruder so much information. House sitting implied Kent wasn't home. Maybe if I hadn't been half-asleep, I would have had enough common sense to lie and say Kent was in the house.

The man jerked his dark eyes around the room. "Where's Marian?"

I bent my knees, preparing for a hundred-mile-per-hour sprint to the door, when a flash of silver in his right hand caught my eye. It was a pistol.

I yanked my arm free and ran from him at the fastest pace my rubbery legs would allow. I made it halfway to the front door before he grabbed my shoulder.

He spun me around to face him, bringing me close to his red, sweat-soaked face. The man looked to be in his late-thirties, maybe older, with near-black eyes and matching hair cropped in an angular, military style. "I said, tell me where Marian is."

"I don't know," I shrieked. "I met her for the first time yesterday afternoon. She stopped by on her way to the dry cleaners."

"How long have you been staying with Kent?"

"I met him on Sunday and started working—"

The man gave a sharp laugh. "Wow. You've known Kent several days and now you're sleeping at his house. Figures."

"It's not like that." I twisted and squirmed, trying to free myself from his grasp. "He hired me to redesign his outdoor living—"

"I've heard this one before. Why do think Marian divorced me a year ago? She worked for him, too, before she walked out on me. Does Marian know Kent is cheating on her with you?"

The man released my arm and stuffed his gun into the back of his jeans, then took several steps back. I wanted to bolt, but the man had caught up to me so quickly a moment ago that I didn't have much hope of outrunning him.

Even without a gun in his hand, he was intimidating. A thin red T-shirt stretched taut across his bulky arms and chest, telling me he spent a lot of time in the gym. And considering how profusely he was sweating, he looked like he was fired up on enough adrenaline to power an entire football team. He could probably outrun a cheetah at the moment.

"He's not cheating on her," I said, keeping my voice as calm as possible. "Kent hired me to spiff up his backyard for Marian's surprise birthday party. I'm an interior designer, but I agreed to watch his house and dog, Chip, while he's out of town."

At the sound of his name, Chip hopped down from sofa, pranced over to the man, and sat on his haunches, his tail swishing slowly.

Why wasn't he barking? He barked at everyone.

"Who are you?" I asked.

"Phillip Koh. Marian's hus—I mean, ex-husband." He backed up a few more steps and sat on the arm of Kent's sofa. "I'm looking for Marian. One of her coworkers called me this morning and said she's missing. I can't reach her either, so I drove all the way from North Carolina today to look for her."

"Have you spoken with her recently?" I asked. "Do you have any idea where she may have gone? Maybe someone made her angry?"

Someone like me, who was floating in her fiancé's pool?

"She's not the type to run away without telling anyone. Not Marian. She's too headstrong to let anyone run her off."

I glanced past Phillip at the open window through which he'd entered, wishing he would leave. My heart was hammering wildly and my hands were so shaky, I probably wouldn't even be able to unlock the front door to escape. Taking a deep breath, I refocused on Phillip. He claimed he wanted to find Marian, so maybe he would leave if I suggested some logical places to look for her.

"You said Marian works for Kent?" I confirmed. "Maybe she decided to surprise him in Philly on his business trip and didn't tell anyone."

"No, she used to work for him. Marian is a financial advisor and Kent's small electronics company was one of her clients." His expression soured. "The two of them have been together ever since she flew to Australia with him on a 'business trip' to help him with his 'overseas investment portfolio.' I should have known it was more than a coincidence he asked her to accompany him on a trip down yonder, which just so happens to be her favorite place."

My eyes shifted to the window again. "Even if Marian doesn't still work for Kent, I'd bet she's on her way to visit him in Philly. Maybe her flight was delayed and she's still at the airport. You should go check, see if she's there."

Phillip turned around, following my gaze. He stood abruptly and adjusted his gun in his jeans. "You know as well as I do Marian is not hanging out at the airport." He strode to the window and stepped through it with his left leg, then snapped his dark eyes over to me. "Do not tell anyone I was here tonight. If you know what's good for you, you'll keep your mouth shut."

As soon as Phillip was on the other side of the window, I ran toward it and locked it, then scurried around and checked all of the windows on the first floor.

If I know what's good for me? What was that supposed to mean? It sounded like something an angry teacher would say—or perhaps an angry ex-husband who didn't want me putting my nose where it didn't belong.

I snatched my phone from the coffee table and hurried to the staircase where I could consider my options. I wasn't going to stand around in the middle of the family room, with its wall-to-wall windows. At this point, I didn't know who was on the outside looking in.

Looking down at my phone, I considered calling the officer I'd met earlier today. He would probably like to know Marian's ex-husband had come into Kent's home with a gun. But Phillip's words still rang in my ears. Was he threatening me? Or did he think someone else might harm me if I spoke up?

I sat at the top of the stairs, cowering in the shadows. If I had my car with me, I would load up my bag and Chip and drive over to Aunt Deb's.

I checked the time. It was 12:30 a.m. Kent would be home in

several hours and then I could high-tail it over to Aunt Deb's. Even though I was running away from a bad breakup, I wouldn't run from my first client in Darlington Hills, no matter how badly I wanted to leave his house.

Turning around, I surveyed the dark hallway upstairs. I could hide out in the guest bedroom until Kent arrived, but there was no way I'd be able to go back to sleep after what had just happened.

My eyes landed on the door to Kent's upstairs office. Why had Officer Appley been so eager to see what was inside? Did he think the room held clues to Marian's location?

I drummed my fingers rapidly against the carpeted step. Kent kept the door locked for a reason. He was my client and it was my responsibility to respect his privacy. But Marian was his fiancée and he desperately wanted her to return safely.

Whatever was in the room, whatever business files he kept locked away, couldn't be more important than finding Marian. I doubted anything in there would lead the police to her, but it was worth taking a peek inside.

And I felt partly responsible for Marian's disappearance. Three people I'd talked with in the past twenty-four hours— Celine, Officer Appley, and now Phillip—had assumed I was staying at Kent's because I was involved with him romantically. It was logical to think Marian had come to the same conclusion, and then run off because of anger and hurt.

I needed to find her and help fix things, and I had something the police didn't have at the moment: access to Kent's office.

Recalling Officer Appley's not-so-subtle breaking-and-entering advice of using a hairpin to unlock the door, I lowered myself to the next step, then another and another until I reached the bottom of the stairs.

I headed to the kitchen and searched Kent's drawers, but didn't find any long, straight objects that would fit through the hole in the door handle.

Maybe Kent's bathroom? Marian had come by the house yesterday to pick up her dress for dry cleaning; maybe she kept other personal items like hairpins at Kent's.

I peeked around the corner of the wall separating the kitchen and family room, scanning the large black windows to make sure no one was staring back at me. Then I sprinted through the room to Kent's bedroom. Chip followed me, his tail wagging wildly as though we were playing tag.

"This is not a game," I informed him. "It's strictly police business. Except neither of us are on the force."

This made him bark with delight, and he followed me around as I peeked inside all of the dresser drawers. Finding nothing, I moved into the bathroom.

There were two sink areas, each with half a dozen drawers and cabinets on either side. I aimed for the sink that wasn't cluttered with manly toiletries and opened the top drawer. A large black and white floral bag lay atop a slew of make-up and accessories. I dug through a collection of hair brushes, nail polish, cotton balls, and tube upon tube of lip gloss until I found a hairpin. I slid it into the pocket of my shorts and closed the drawer.

Then I reopened it, along with all of the other drawers and cabinets surrounding Marian's sink area. I was already guilty of snooping, and there wasn't much difference between a little snooping and a lot.

Most of the drawers were empty, other than the one with the make-up and another one on the bottom that contained two small ceramic cats. Marian had made it clear she didn't care for dogs, but the figurines told me she was more of a cat person.

Removing the floral bag from the make-up drawer, I unzipped it and peeked inside. There was a collection of half-used shampoo, conditioner, and lotion bottles from various hotels. I pulled them out one by one and set them on the countertop. Most were from ritzy hotel chains in which I had never stayed.

"Here's some lotion from a hotel in London," I told Chip as I unscrewed the top of the bottle and took a whiff. It smelled every bit as expensive as its name sounded.

I removed another bottle from the bag, unscrewed its top and held it under my nose. It had a pleasant aroma, one I liked more than the one from London.

Turning the bottle around, I read its label: Cucumber Mint Medley Hand Cream by Hotel Darlington.

I frowned. Why would Marian stay at a local hotel when she lived here?

There were five other bottles of the same cucumber mint hand cream in her bag, all half-used. My heart thudded with hope. From the looks of it, Marian had stayed at Hotel Darlington multiple times. Maybe it was where she went when she needed to get away; maybe she was there now.

I stuffed the bottles back in the bag, returned it to the drawer, then switched off the light to the bathroom. Tomorrow I'd stop by Hotel Darlington and look for Marian. I would try to make things right.

But tonight, I would look inside Kent's upstairs office, if only to win another dimpled smile from the cute officer.

As I climbed the stairs once again, I brainstormed excuses for why I needed to go in there, just in case Kent found out.

I pulled the hairpin from my pocket. Maybe I could use Officer Appley's excuse that I needed office supplies. I could say I needed a hole-puncher so I could add paper to the design binder for his backyard project.

Nope. Too weak of an excuse. Kent likely had plenty of office supplies downstairs.

I aligned the hairpin with the tiny hole in the handle and slid it inside, searching for any buttons to click. Perhaps I could blame it on Officer Appley. I could say he told me to do it.

I sighed. That excuse wouldn't work either. Not only did it

sound like something a tattling toddler would say, but it might also get Officer Appley in trouble.

Without any believable excuses, I would have to be extra careful not to leave any evidence of my office visit. There was a soft click. I pulled down on the handle and the door cracked open. Chip pressed his nose against the door and pushed it wide enough for him to walk through.

"Chip! Come back here," I whispered, suddenly regretting my decision to unlock the door.

A soft scraping noise came from inside the dark room, making my heart thud faster. What had Chip found?

I stepped inside the room and felt alongside the adjacent wall until I touched the light switch and flipped it.

My eyes widened as I surveyed the room. Bold, zebra-striped wallpaper covered all four walls while leopard-print curtains hung to the sides of a small window in middle of the wall opposite the door. Framed photos of kangaroos, koalas, crocodiles, zebras, and emus hung at evenly spaced intervals, all at my eye-level. The office was an eclectic mix of Australian outback and African safari, channeling both Crocodile Dundee and Indiana Jones.

To my left, there was a small table by the window, rolling office chair, and four-drawer file cabinet, which held the phone that rang incessantly last night. A large antique wooden armoire stood against the wall directly in front of me. To its left was a corduroy dog bed, on which Chip gnawed at a half-chewed rawhide bone. He looked like he was in his happy place.

"Don't get too comfortable," I told Chip. "We're not staying in here long."

He paused to look at me with his one-eyed stare, then resumed chewing his bone. I hurried over to the file cabinet and pulled on its four drawer handles. All were locked.

I'd already picked one lock tonight and I wasn't about to try to break into any others. I looked at the table and office chair.

Both were covered in a thick layer of dust, telling me he didn't use the room as an office.

Careful not to touch the table and leave any fingerprints in the dust, I leaned over to look inside the trash can that sat under the table. There was a wadded-up paper towel and a broken ceramic kangaroo, similar to the cat figurine I'd seen in the bathroom drawer downstairs.

"Your daddy sure loves knick-knacks," I said to Chip.

I crossed the room and opened the sliding door to the closet. There was a stack of baseball caps and several thick winter coats, but the shelves were otherwise empty.

Closing the doors, I eyed a framed photo of a kangaroo mid-leap on the wall to my left. Like the other photos in the room, this one was an incredible action shot. I was curious if Kent had taken the photos, but it wasn't a question I'd ever ask him.

I headed for the wooden armoire. The doors had intricately carved floral designs and forged brass hardware, both with a keyhole just above the knob.

There was a good chance it was locked, but I pulled on the knob anyway. The door creaked as it swung open, as though it were protesting my snooping.

I blinked rapidly, trying to make sense of what I was staring at. Or, rather, what was staring back at me.

Three shelves held dozens of different ceramic kangaroo figurines arranged in perfect rows, spaced precisely three inches apart. Most were brown, some white or gray, and all of them faced forward, aiming their dark beady eyes at me.

Below each kangaroo were small bronze plates engraved with a name. I swept my eyes across the nameplates directly in front of me: Paula, Brittany, Princess, Molly, Rhonda. There was one kangaroo missing from the top shelf, which according to the nameplate, was named Mary Lou. I wondered if Mary Lou was the unfortunate kangaroo in the trash can.

I lifted Rhonda the kangaroo and turned her over in my

hands as I studied her. She was light brown with white legs, and had a tiny gold 'Made in China' sticker on her belly.

I looked at Chip, as if he would be able to explain why Kent had such a vast collection of named kangaroos.

Phillip had said Australia was Marian's favorite place in the world. Were kangaroos her favorite animal? Had she decorated this room? Maybe this was her collection.

But this was more than a collection. It was an obsession. And someone wanted to keep it hidden behind a locked door.

CHAPTER SEVEN

For the next two hours, I sat at the top of the stairs, out of sight from anyone who may be peering in through the windows. I was wide awake, even though I'd gotten less than three hours of sleep before Phillip came through the window.

I prayed Kent's plane would arrive early so I could crawl into Aunt Deb's guest bed and get a few hours of sleep before my job interview at Walnut Ridge. Seven-thirty on a Saturday morning was insanely early for an interview, but I hadn't complained because the owner was working me into his schedule after canceling the first interview.

Chip lay next to me, and I took comfort in the fact he was sleeping quietly instead of barking at mystery shadows. One peep from him would have sent me back into panic mode. I was done with the drama surrounding this house. Kent's plane could not arrive fast enough.

At 3:10 a.m., my phone's screen lit up with a text from Kent. He had landed and was on his way home. Forty-five minutes later, a low rumble sounded downstairs as the garage door opened.

After leaving my suitcase and handbag by the front door, I

met Kent by the utility room as he came inside the house. The smiling, upbeat man I remembered from less than a week ago now had unkempt hair and drooping shoulders, which I took as a sign he hadn't received any word on Marian.

I wanted to share with him my theory that Marian had perhaps gone to Hotel Darlington for some time to herself while she fumed about finding me in the pool, but that would mean I'd have to confess to finding the bottles of hotel hand cream while snooping through his bathroom.

"Here, let me help you with these," I said, reaching for a small overnight bag dangling from his thumb.

"Thanks, Hadley. You don't know how much I appreciate you helping out while I've been gone. Especially these last couple of days."

He pulled his rolling suitcase inside the house, then dumped the remaining items in his arms—an empty fast-food bag, water bottle, and folded newspaper—onto the washing machine.

I followed him into the kitchen, where he tossed his keys into the drawer under the microwave. He didn't seem to notice the faint smell of burnt eggs, or if he did, he didn't say anything. I had kept the windows open until Aunt Deb left, but I still caught an occasional whiff of the stench.

"Listen, it's late and you're welcome to stay here until morning if you'd like," he said. "You look like you could use some more sleep."

I rocked back on my heels and stole a quick glimpse of my reflection in the kitchen window. Yikes. Not only did I need more sleep, I also needed a shower, blow dryer, flat iron, and mascara before I met with the owner of Walnut Ridge.

"Thanks, but I'm going to call a cab. I've already packed up my stuff and my aunt is expecting me at her place."

He pulled his brows together. "She's waiting up for you at this hour?"

"No, but I have a job interview in a few hours and I really should get going."

Kent put his palms up and stepped back as though he were surrendering. "If you insist. But please let me take you to your aunt's; it's the least I can do after you've been so helpful. My truck has plenty of gas and I won't be able to sleep tonight anyway. Not until I know Marian is safe."

Instead of retrieving his truck keys from the kitchen drawer, he turned around and walked out of the room. "Give me two minutes. I'll be right back." The steady thuds of Kent's feet on the stairs made my thoughts lurch from one worry to another.

Would he know I went into his office? Would he fire me if he found out?

A door opened, then closed. I slipped into the entry hall and listened. He was rustling something upstairs, but I couldn't tell which room he was in. Earlier, before I left the office and locked the door, I triple checked to make sure I left everything exactly the way it was when I entered. I'd even dried the bone Chip had chewed on.

Had I missed something?

I climbed the first three stairs and aimed my ear toward the hallway upstairs. There were three beeps, followed by a woman's voice.

It was the shrill, impatient voice of Marian's roommate, Celine. Kent *was* in his upstairs office, listening to his voicemail. How peculiar that a man who owned an electronics company still used an answering machine. Maybe he collected old machines like he collected figurines.

The door opened again, prompting me to sail over the bottom three steps in one adrenaline-fueled jump and hustle back to the kitchen. Kent padded down the hallway toward the stairs.

"Hadley?" he called out.

"In here," I said, trying to keep my voice steady. I moved

slowly back into the entry hall. My hands became damp as I waited for his return.

Kent came into view as he descended the stairs. "When Marian's roommate came over, did she say whether they got into another argument?"

I shook my head.

"Did she seem angry or agitated?"

"Yes, she was upset. She was worried about Marian."

"Interesting," he said dryly.

The doorbell rang and we both spun around. Kent strode forward and looked through the peephole. His fingers raced to unlock the door and turn the knob. He swung open the door.

Officer Appley stood on the other side, his eyes void of the smile they'd held when I met him yesterday afternoon. Behind him, the street lit up with the swirling red and blue lights from Officer Appley's patrol car.

He held up his badge. "Officer Dennis Appley. Are you Mr. Reading? May I come in?"

Kent opened the door wider and stepped back to allow Officer Appley enough space to enter. "Yes, I'm Kent. Do you have any news about Marian?"

Officer Appley kept his somber gaze on Kent. "I'm sorry, Mr. Reading, but one of our officers located your fiancée about an hour ago. Her body was found in Bonn Creek near the eastern footbridge. Our detective is at the scene right now as this is a suspected homicide case."

CHAPTER EIGHT

"Tell me why I should hire you as Walnut Ridge's interior designer. How would you help take my company to the next level?" Vincent Weatherford, owner of Walnut Ridge Furniture and Decor, leaned back in his chair and tapped a ballpoint pen against the table in his breakfast nook. With mostly gray hair, a trim gray and black goatee, and minimal wrinkles, I placed him in his late thirties or early forties.

Unlike Vincent, who wore a white polo shirt and dark blue jeans, I had dressed up for the interview, opting for a tailored black dress and heels.

Behind Vincent there was a beautiful, sparkling white kitchen adorned with numerous accessories—glass bulbous vases, champagne-gold pendant lights, various serving bowls—all of which I'd recently become familiar with when I researched his company's products online.

Vincent had bought the house and moved to Darlington Hills less than a year ago. Not only was it his personal home, it was also the Walnut Ridge Home, in which one very lucky interior designer would have the opportunity to stage rooms with the company's furniture and accessories for photoshoots for the new catalog.

I wanted this job. Not only so I could escape the city overrun with billboard-sized photos of my ex-boyfriend, but because I wanted to settle down in a town I could call home.

As the daughter of an Air Force airman, I lived in eight different southern cities before my parents dropped me off at college. I was tired of moving. I wanted to find my forever town where I could grow my roots one friendship at a time. Darlington Hills seemed like the perfect place to unload my final moving truck. It was a fairytale town, apart from the devastating death of Marian, which weighed as heavily on my heart as it did my mind.

Taking a deep breath, I pushed aside the memory of Kent's crumpled face when Officer Appley told him about Marian. I had to focus on my interview.

"I would be an asset to your company because I've gained valuable experience as a designer for a custom home builder in New Orleans, where I not only style their model homes but also help customers make design selections for paint, flooring, lighting and hardware. If you look through the online portfolio I emailed you, you'll find that my style of southern—fresh, contemporary, inspired-by-nature—aligns perfectly with Walnut Ridge's product line."

I straightened my back and put a fresh smile on my face. "I know there are other interior designers who also have relevant work experience and portfolios. What I would bring to your company is a jolt of passion that motivates me to work until I'm one hundred percent happy with every detail of the project."

Vincent scribbled something on the yellow notepad in front of him, then looked up at me with raised eyebrows, as though I hadn't quite answered his question. "If you're so accomplished in your current job, why are you leaving it?"

It was a question I had prepared for, though I hadn't anticipated it would carry such a condescending undertone. "While I feel a sense of accomplishment with what I have achieved in my current job, I am seeking another opportunity to challenge myself further. And I believe I can be a meaningful part of Walnut Ridge's plans for expansion by helping to position the company as the leading supplier of contemporary southern home furnishings. I'd love to be part of your company's future success."

He grunted. "That's the response everyone gives. What's the real reason you want to move here? Bad boss? Pay cut? Running from a bunch of unpaid parking tickets?"

"No. I'm running from a broken heart." I gave a tight smile, hoping the 'honesty is the best policy' maxim held true in job interviews with grumpy owners of home furnishing companies.

Vincent barked out a laugh. "Why would you run from a lively city like New Orleans to *this* place? I've lived here less than a year, and nothing ever happens in Darlington Hills. This place is like an eternal yawn."

"I've been in town for less than a week, and I've encountered more drama than I ever did in New Orleans."

"Oh? Did someone knock over a neighbor's flower pot?"

I cringed inwardly, wishing I hadn't brought up the subject of Marian's death during my job interview. But I'd already dug the hole and it was too late to try to climb out of it, and Vincent would hear the news about her death eventually, if he hadn't already. "Do you know Marian Koh?"

"No. Should I?"

"She lives on—*lived* on the east side of Darlington Hills. She went missing late Thursday night, then the police found her body earlier this morning in Bonn Creek."

Vincent flinched. "That's awful. I'm sorry to hear that." He paused, seeming to consider what I'd just told him. His brows drew closer together. "How do you know about this? You said they found her earlier this morning? It's not even eight o'clock yet."

"Because I'm working on an interior design job for Marian's fiancé. I'm redoing his outdoor living space."

The line between his eyebrows deepened. "You have a client here? In Darlington Hills? Was this something you arranged before you traveled here?"

"No, I met him at a local café last Sunday and started working for him on Monday. And while we're on the subject, I should mention that I'm planning to continue my interior design side business, Hadley Home Design, in whichever town I move. But I can assure you it wouldn't interfere with my day job, which takes precedence over my client work."

He swished my comment away with his hand as though it weren't a big deal. Thank goodness. It was important to me to have a boss who would support me having a side business.

What I didn't tell Vincent was that I hoped Hadley Home Design would someday become so successful that I wouldn't need to work for someone else and could rely entirely on income from clients.

Vincent still seemed deep in thought. "So your new client called you in the middle of the night to tell you about the death of his fiancée?"

"He's been keeping me posted on everything because he knows I care," I replied, hoping my vague answer was sufficient. I wanted to avoid any more scandalous assumptions about why I had stayed at Kent's house.

Again, images of Kent's tear-streaked face flashed through my mind as I recalled Officer Appley's devastating report. He'd told Kent an officer found Marian shortly after midnight when following up on a call from a young man who had spotted a body in the creek while walking his dog late at night.

Both Kent and I provided a statement to Officer Appley, during which he pulled us individually into Kent's downstairs office while he scribbled onto a notepad. I told him about my venture into Kent's upstairs office, but withheld the part about

Phillip's intrusion. As much as I didn't want to admit it, Phillip's threat scared me, and I didn't want to find out what would happen if I told the police.

After Officer Appley took our statements, he gave me a ride to Aunt Deb's on his way back to the station. He told me to call if I needed anything and said he or the detective would be in touch if they had any follow-up questions.

Now, sitting in the sun-lit breakfast area of the Walnut Ridge home, last night's tragedy seemed like a distant nightmare.

Vincent asked me three more classic interview questions—my greatest strengths, greatest weaknesses, and what I like to do outside of work. I played up my strengths, highlighting my strong work ethic and dedication to keeping up with the latest trends in interior design, downplayed my greatest weakness, telling him I have trouble saying no to more work projects. I'd read on a career advice website that this was a good response for the weakness question because it shows both self-awareness and your willingness to take on more work.

I then described my hobbies, but only named my top three—cooking, antique shopping, and hanging out with friends—because I didn't get the sense he was genuinely interested in my response. He had likely found his interview questions on some of the same websites where I found my responses.

Vincent checked his watch, then put the cap back on his pen. "I have a meeting with a contractor in twenty minutes, so we need to wrap this up. One more important question before you leave."

I leaned forward, smiling pleasantly. One more question. I could do this.

"If a snail is at the bottom of a nine-foot wall and he climbs eleven inches every day but slides back down two-and-a-half inches in the evening, how long does it take him to reach the top?"

I froze. Did he really just ask me a math question? What was he trying to gauge by my answer? My personality? My ability to tackle difficult problems head-on? Surely it wasn't my math skills he cared about.

I decided to keep my answer relevant to my expertise, which most definitely did not include solving complicated math problems in my head.

"Well, if the snail employed me as his interior designer, I would have the wall recovered with a texturized wallpaper that would prevent him from slipping. It is a designer's responsibility to not only make living spaces aesthetically pleasing, but also functional. And a wall that doesn't provide enough traction for the poor snail lacks basic functionality." I grinned, relieved I had gotten past that beast of a question.

Vincent sighed. "You sidestepped my question, Hadley. I asked you to solve a math problem. Interior designers use simple math in their jobs, do they not? Calculations for area, geometry, and such?"

I pulled back my chin. Vincent was becoming more condescending by the minute. He must be a real gem of a boss to work for.

"So I'll ask you again, if a snail is at the bottom of a nine-foot wall and he climbs eleven inches every day but slides back down two-and-a-half inches in the evening, how long does it take him to reach the top?"

"Well, if the wallpaper has proper traction and the snail doesn't slip, then it would take him a little more than nine—"

"Forget about re-wallpapering," he snapped. "Can you or can't you answer my question?"

I had two options: run away as fast as I could from the horrid math question and demeaning owner of Walnut Ridge, or admit defeat. If Vincent was more concerned with my math skills than design expertise, then this wasn't the job for me. And I may have been running from New Orleans, but I wasn't going to give up on this job opportunity.

Turning my palms up, I gave him a sheepish smile. "I'm sorry, but I don't know the answer. I did fine in my math courses, but solving math problems like this one in my head is not one of my strengths."

Vincent slid back his chair, stood, and motioned to the front of his house. "Thank you for meeting with me this morning. I believe I have everything I need. I will inform you of my decision within a week."

I rose and shook his hand, then followed him to the door. "And thank you for considering me as a candidate for your open position. I'm heading out to breakfast now to eat some escargot."

CHAPTER NINE

I needed coffee. I didn't want to think about snails or moody owners of home furnishing companies, or how badly I'd blown my job interview.

Even on a typical day, when I'd had plenty of rest and wasn't reeling from the sudden news of a homicide, I still wouldn't have been able to work out Vincent's math equation without using a calculator or paper.

I had felt prepared for my interview. I'd researched possible questions, practiced my responses, and I had sacrificed an extra hour of sleep to flat iron my hair and put on extra makeup. Unfortunately, I had failed to brush up on my algebra skills.

After leaving Vincent's home, I headed toward the town square for some coffee. Aunt Deb was out hiking this morning, as she did most mornings. She headed up the town's hiking club, leading several dozen women around the woodsy regions of Darlington Hills five days of the week. Had she been home, I would have gone there to talk.

I looked at the pavement ahead and used a hand to shield my eyes from the sharp rays of the low-angled sun. Aunt Deb had dropped me off at Vincent's before her hike, and I had planned to call a cab afterwards to spare my feet from walking back in heels.

But now I didn't want to call a cab. I needed to walk off my worries. My head was a swirling mess of thoughts about the job interview and Marian's death.

As I approached Bonn Creek and the footbridge connecting the northern and southern sections of Darlington Hills, I increased my pace. Although Officer Appley had said police found Marian's body in the creek by the other footbridge—the one on the east side of town—I couldn't bear to look into the water below.

Even before Marian's death, spooky legends and darkness surrounded Bonn Creek, or as locals called it, Bone Creek. Darlington Hills was settled in the 1700s, but the town was originally named Bonnville after the wealthy colonist Charles Bonn, who emigrated with forty-nine members of his extended family and claimed stake to this area north of the James River in current-day Virginia.

According to the legend, all but one member of the Bonn family drowned in the creek that divided the two sides of town. To this day, there were rumors that descendants of the sole survivor still lived in the area, but no one knew for sure if this was true. The town's name was changed in the mid-1800s because of the harrowing events surrounding the Bonn family name. Bonnville became Darlington Hills, named after the numerous native Darlington oak trees in the area.

These stories about the Bonn family tragedy had been as much a part of my childhood as *Little Red Riding Hood* and the *Three Little Pigs*. During my visits to Darlington Hills, my cousin Michael used to enjoy spooking me with Bonn tales, always right before I went to sleep.

Ten minutes later, my heels hit the smooth cobblestone pavers that spanned the entire town square, and I clip-clopped my way toward Erin's Whisks and Whiskers Cat Café.

A cheerful chime announced my entry when I opened the door. Two kittens on a nearby carpeted play structure turned their heads in my direction, half-closing their eyes at the cold breeze I brought in with me.

Heading for an open chair at the coffee bar, I waved to Erin, who was carrying an armful of dirty dishes toward the double doors leading to the kitchen. She acknowledged me with a grim smile. She must've already heard about Marian.

A waiter in a black Whisks and Whiskers apron approached me. I guessed he was a junior or senior in high school.

He offered me a wide grin. "Mornin', miss. What can I get you?"

"I'd like a vanilla latte, please, along with a blueberry muffin." Glancing at his name tag, I pulled some cash from my purse and handed it to him. "Thanks, Peter."

"You got it. One vanilla latte and blueberry muffin for the newest face in town." Peter turned and pulled a white mug from the shelf behind him, then looked back at me from the corner of his eye. "Although I swear I've seen you before. Have you lived here long?"

I returned his smile. "Nope, just visiting. But I was in here last Sunday."

He shook his head. "I'm off on Sundays, so I must have seen you around somewhere else."

It was doubtful, considering I'd spent the majority of the past week at Kent's house.

Erin came through the kitchen doors holding a slice of quiche. She set it down in front of a woman sitting next to me.

"I said I wanted the spinach quiche, not the ham and cheese one," the woman said, pushing the dish away.

Erin's hands trembled as she lifted the plate. "I'm sorry, Mrs. Little. I'll bring your broccoli quiche out in just a few—"

"*Spinach* quiche." Mrs. Little corrected. "Not broccoli, not onions, definitely not ham, but spinach. In fact, I'd like a to-go bag for it, because I'm going to eat it at home. I can see you're rather busy in here this morning, and it's gonna make my blood pressure rise."

"Of course. I'll get you a take-home bag, and for the inconvenience I caused you, I'm going to throw in some Fur-rocious Fish Niblets for your sweet Mittens."

Mrs. Littles' face softened. "Thank you, dear. Those fish niblets are Mittens' favorite. Nowadays if I come home with a bag of any sort, she thinks it's filled with cat treats."

Erin apologized once again and returned to the kitchen with the unwanted quiche. Mrs. Little turned toward me. "You have any cats? If so, you must buy a bag of fish niblets. Cats will do anything for those treats. I swear I could teach my Mittens to sweep the floors and do my laundry if I bribed her with enough of them."

I laughed. "I don't have any pets right now, but I may adopt one if I move here." If Vincent hired me, which at the moment seemed unlikely.

"Well then, speaking on behalf of my fellow Darlington Hills friends and family, we would welcome you with open arms to our little town." She paused, narrowing her eyes. "I believe I know you from somewhere. Forgive me if we've already met, but what is your name again?"

"Hadley Sutton," I said, fighting the temptation to roll my eyes at yet another case of familiar face mistaken identity. First the waiter and now Mrs. Little—two times in less than five minutes. This could be a new record.

Mrs. Littles' eyes ignited with recognition. "Sutton! You're Deb's niece—and Brady's daughter! You look just like him. I grew up with your father and was so disappointed when he moved away after high school. He was a real charmer around here. Oh, and I rent a unit from your aunt's mini storage facility, which is an absolute godsend for organizationally challenged folks like myself."

An orange and white tabby cat rubbed against my leg, then looked at me and gave a loud, authoritative meow.

"Hey there, kitty," I said, even though the tabby had clearly passed the kitten stage years ago. It was the largest cat in the café, and I guessed it ate more than its fair share of fish niblets.

"That's King Oliver," Mrs. Little informed me as I reached over and scratched the top of his head. "He's Erin's personal cat; the only one in here who isn't available for adoption. And he certainly lives up to his name. You should see the way he swaggers around this place, turning his nose up at anyone who doesn't kowtow to him."

Mrs. Little stood when Erin returned with a white paper bag. "Thank you, dear. And Mittens will thank you, too."

As soon as Mrs. Little walked away, Erin pressed her fingertips to her eyes and released a long sigh. "Have you heard about Marian?" she asked, keeping her voice low. "I read about it in the *Darlington Hills Dispatch* this morning."

I nodded. "I was at Kent's house when the police notified him. He'd just gotten home from his trip and was getting ready to take me to my aunt's when the officer knocked on the door."

Erin's eyes shifted around the café. "My boyfriend, Rhett, tried calling Kent an hour ago to see if he needs anything, but he didn't pick up. I guess he's not ready to take condolence calls from coworkers yet."

I nodded. "He probably needs some time to himself."

Peter placed my latte and muffin down in front of me, then slid a tiny pitcher of coffee creamer next to my mug. "Let me know if I can get you anything else."

"I'd like one more muffin, but please put it in a to-go bag," I said. "I'm going to bring it home to my aunt." I handed him a few more dollars, but Erin waved it off and whispered to Peter that it was on the house.

"Thank you," I mouthed to her, bringing the mug of frothy goodness to my lips. "What did the newspaper say?"

Erin's eyes shifted from the countertop to the windows to the coffee machine, never seeming to focus on anything for more than a second. She leaned closer to me. "The story mentioned a gunshot wound. Someone shot her, Hadley. Or she shot herself. The detective they quoted was quite vague. He didn't say much other than they're investigating the cause of death."

My throat felt tight and I had to strain to suck in a full breath. It was devastating to think the woman who had stormed into Kent's backyard three days ago had been found dead in a nearby creek. The gunshot wound explained why Officer Appley said it was a suspected homicide.

"Who would do such a thing?" I whispered.

She snapped her gaze abruptly to the front of the café, where an older man in plaid shorts was coming through the door. "I can't imagine anyone around here killing her. It might've had something to do with her business. She was a financial advisor, so maybe she gave someone bad advice and they lost a lot of money."

Taking another sip, I considered that scenario. The day I met Marian, she had returned from a business trip early. Maybe she'd had a bad meeting with a client and left because she felt threatened. It seemed possible, but not likely. I continued to worry Marian's disappearance and now death had something to do with her finding me in Kent's pool. As much as I tried to reassure myself it didn't, my heart was still heavy with guilt. Even if Marian hadn't run off because she thought Kent was cheating on her, I deeply regretted not telling her about the surprise birthday party.

If Marian had known why Kent had kept the patio redesign a secret, maybe she would've done something differently the night she disappeared. Maybe she would have had other plans that didn't result in her death. Or, if nothing else, maybe she would have died without thinking Kent was cheating on her.

I set down my mug, sending a small dollop of froth over the

edge and onto the countertop. Erin plucked a napkin from the dispenser. The thin white paper fluttered in her shaking hands as she dabbed at my mess.

"Sorry about the spill," I said. The side of her hand hit the small pitcher of coffee creamer, nearly tipping it over. She lifted the pitcher and moved it away from the area she was cleaning.

"Are you okay?" I asked. "I know this must be especially hard on you." Erin's hands shook so much that she seemed to be having a hard time holding the pitcher.

She followed my gaze to her hands, then set the pitcher down hastily and stuffed them into the front pockets of her apron. "I'm fine," she said quickly. "I haven't known Marian very long; I met her the same day you did."

"I just meant this must be even more upsetting to you and your boyfriend since he works for Kent."

"Oh. Right. Yes, we're both still in shock." She nodded toward the tables in the café. "Listen, we're busier than usual today, and one of my baristas called in sick, so I need to get back to work. But thanks for coming by this morning. You'll have to tell me how your job interview went sometime when things settle down."

Erin gave me a quick smile, then turned her attention to a man who sat down next to me. I'd only known her for a week, but it was long enough to know she was clearly shaken by Marian's death.

King Oliver marched over to a two-tiered cat structure, hopped onto the top level, and with one loud meow, convinced a white Siamese-tabby cat to give up her spot. King Oliver's long orange tail swished furiously, as though he were warning the other cats not to enter his domain. Even King Oliver seemed uptight this morning.

CHAPTER TEN

I waved goodbye to Erin before I pushed open the café's door and stepped outside. The sun was higher now, but there was still a crisp chill in the air. Bolstered by an extra dose of caffeine, I was ready to face the day.

Before Officer Appley delivered the news of Marian's death, I had planned to finalize Kent's patio area this weekend. There were several more deliveries scheduled, mostly smaller accessories to tie in the broader style and color themes. But now I would need to cancel them once the stores opened in an hour or so.

The patio redesign would be the furthest thing on Kent's mind this morning, and I didn't want him having to deal with crews delivering patio decor.

I considered my options: I could go back to Aunt Deb's house and wait for her to come home. I wanted to spend more time with her before I flew home Monday night, especially since there was a significant chance I wouldn't get the job at Walnut Ridge, thanks to the math question.

But I wasn't quite ready to go back to Aunt Deb's. I couldn't get the bottle of cucumber mint hand cream out of my mind, and

I had forgotten to mention it to Officer Appley when he questioned me last night.

I didn't know if it was relevant to the investigation, but it was odd that Marian appeared to frequent a local hotel when she had her own house in town. It didn't make sense.

The only way to alleviate the sharp sting of guilt for not being completely honest with Marian was to search for answers.

First things first, I needed to go to Hotel Darlington. I owed it to Marian to help figure out how she died.

I shifted the white paper bag holding Aunt Deb's blueberry muffin to my left hand, then pulled my phone from my handbag, opened my map app, and typed in Hotel Darlington. The app dinged and beeped, informing me it would take eight minutes to reach my destination by foot. Obviously, the app wasn't accounting for the fact I was walking in heels.

"Turn right onto Sundale Avenue," said the pleasant computer voice.

I did as instructed, heading east through the stone-paved town square along Sundale Avenue. To my left, a large circular water foundation was positioned in the middle of the square.

When I'd visited the square last weekend with Aunt Deb, it had been bustling with early springtime energy. But the square was nearly empty today, and those who were present didn't linger to sit on the perimeter of the fountain to sip their coffee as they had last week.

Instead, they strolled through the area with quick strides and downward gazes. News of Marian's death must have spread quickly through the small town.

The boutique shops and small restaurants that lined the town square gave way to tall oak trees that loomed overhead, their regal branches providing shade to the cars parked on the side of the road. The subtle scent of oak trees was barely detectable among the bustling smells of the nearby restaurants.

Two blocks past the town square, I turned right onto a street with small office buildings, none more than four or five stories high.

Seven intersections later, the rounded Hotel Darlington sign came into view. Although it was far from a luxury hotel, its grounds were meticulously maintained, with bright green lawns and neat flowerbeds. Pathways were lined with colorful flowers, trees, and shrubs, creating an atmosphere that was both welcoming and inviting.

I cut through a small opening in the waist-high shrubs that bordered the hotel property, then wove between parked cars toward the entrance.

Ahead of me, a man with black hair and a bright orange laptop bag hanging from his shoulder loaded a suitcase into the trunk of a silver sedan.

"Excuse me," I said as I slipped past the man. He turned and looked at me. "Phillip!" I cried, failing to mask my surprise. "What are you doing here?"

Instinctively, my eyes darted to his hands to check for any firearms. Only a black car remote dangled between his fingers.

"I checked in yesterday morning when I came to look for—" He stopped, his voice breaking.

"I'm so sorry to hear about Marian."

He looked at me with red puffy eyes. "I'm the ex-husband, so I'm not supposed to care as much as the next guy, right?" Opening the front door of his car, he placed one leg inside. "But I guarantee you I care more about her than that fiancé of hers did. He didn't know her like I did. And you can tell him that, since you're living with him these days."

"I wasn't living with him," I said, trying not to sound overly defensive. "I left Kent's house as soon as he came back from his trip, and I don't know if I'll see him again. I'm sure he'll put the redesign project on hold."

"Whatever. But if you do see him, ask him what good all his

money is doing him now that she's dead. He won Marian with his fancy home and fat wallet, but right now his money is useless. It won't send her running to him this time." He rested an elbow on top of his car and looked out at the parking lot. "You know how I found out about her death? I read about it in the newspaper left outside my hotel room this morning. Can you believe it? I was married to her for three years and no one bothered to call me. Not one of her friends or family members thought I was worth informing."

I dipped my head. "I'm sorry, it must have been awful to find out that way."

"Of course it was," he snapped. "How did you find out? Kent told you?"

About fifteen yards away, a uniformed doorman greeted an elderly couple who was entering the hotel. I couldn't make out his exact words, but the fact that I could hear him gave me reassurance that he would hear me if I screamed. In the broad daylight, without a gun in Phillip's hand, I didn't feel as threatened as I had last night, but it was best to end our conversation soon. He was becoming more agitated by the second.

"I was getting ready to leave Kent's last night when a police officer came by and informed him of her death."

"You and Kent get a personalized notice of her death and I get nothing," he said, talking through clenched teeth.

I took a step closer to the hotel. "I should get going. Got an errand to run."

"Did the cops question you last night?" Phillip asked.

What he really meant to ask, I knew, was had I told the cops he'd broken into Kent's house with a gun?

"I spoke to the officer when he came over, and he told us they suspect Marian's death was a homicide." It was the best non-answer I could come up with on the fly.

Phillip's upper lip curled. "What kind of cops do they have working in this town? The paper said she had a gunshot wound.

Of course it was a homicide. Marian never would have harmed herself. Never."

"Do you know anyone who disliked her enough to kill her?"

He glanced back at the hotel, then shook his head. "No one comes to mind."

"I don't know if the two of you kept in touch, but can you think of anything out of the ordinary that happened to her recently?"

He leveled two serious eyes at mine. "Yeah, Marian's fiancé invited another woman to spend the week in his house. And what's with all the questions?"

"Just curious," I said.

"It's only a matter of time before the cops start asking me questions; I don't need any more coming from you." Phillip slid into the driver's seat, then reached into the front pocket of his orange laptop bag and removed a pair of sporty-looking mirrored sunglasses. He flipped them onto his head.

"If you're gonna act like a member of a civilian police force, you should start by talking to the little lady who owns *that* place." He motioned to the Whisks and Whiskers logo on the bag with Aunt Deb's muffin.

I pulled my brows together. "Who, Erin? What does she have to do with anything? She met Marian two days ago, the same day I did."

"She has a lot to do with Kent," he said sharply. "Didn't you know she used to date him?"

My mouth fell open, prompting a short laugh from Phillip. "See? Like I said, you should talk to her."

"But she's been dating Rhett, her boyfriend, for a while—I think."

Phillip shrugged. "Don't know. I think there was some overlap." He started to close the car door, but I grabbed it to stop him.

"So what if they dated? Are you suggesting she had something to do with Marian's death?"

Phillip started his car and strapped on his seatbelt. "I don't know the woman. But I do know Kent broke up with her soon after he met Marian. From what I hear, the little lady didn't handle getting dumped well. You'll do yourself a favor by leaving the question-asking to the cops. Folks in this town don't like outsiders snooping around in their business."

CHAPTER ELEVEN

I stepped up to a young woman in a burgundy double-breasted suit jacket standing behind the guest services counter at Hotel Darlington.

"Good morning," I greeted. "I'm hoping you can help me with something. Have you by chance seen this woman at your hotel?" I held up my phone, which featured a photo I'd found of Marian on her company's website.

There was a slim chance they would give me information about their guests, but it was worth a shot. Maybe things worked differently in small-town hotels.

The woman, who looked to be in her early twenties, brushed her stick-straight bangs to one side as she leaned closer and looked at the photo.

Her eyes widened. "She does look familiar. I think she did..." The woman paused, straightening her back and lifting her chin. "Actually, miss, I don't believe I can share information about our guests."

"So she was a guest?" I pressed.

The woman's eyes darted around the service desk. "Yes—well no, I can't confirm that either. I didn't mean to say she's a guest of ours. I just meant..." Glancing over her shoulder, she signaled a young man behind the desk next to her. "Hey, where did Anna go?"

Looking annoyed, the man stopped typing on his computer and covered his phone's mouthpiece. "Break room."

The woman gave me a slight bow. "Please excuse me for a moment. I need to have a chat with my manager."

"Sure, thank you," I said, sweetening my words with a smile. The likelihood of getting any information from the hotel staff was decreasing by the second. But my flight was leaving in two days, and I wanted to at least try to find out whether the bottle of Hotel Darlington hand cream held any significance.

Because I would forever regret doing nothing.

I turned around and scanned the hotel lobby while I waited. Glossy light gray marble floors reflected elaborate crystal chandeliers, which were interspersed throughout the area. The trickling of a waterfall along the far wall balanced nicely with the lively piano music playing over the hotel's speaker system.

Any other day, this would be a comfortable place to relax and read a book and unwind from a hectic week at work. Had Marian come here to relax? Kent had indicated Marian and her roommate Celine got into arguments with each other, so it made sense she would need time away from Celine. But why would she go to a hotel instead of Kent's house?

I caught a subtle whiff of the blueberry muffin in the Whisks and Whiskers' bag, reminding me of what Phillip has said about Erin. Had she really dated Kent? If so, why hadn't she told me? I'd only known her a week, so we weren't exactly best friends, but it seemed like a relevant comment to make while we were floating in his pool.

It was possible Phillip had some of his facts wrong, but I doubted he was completely making it up. He didn't live here, so how would he know the owner of Whisks and Whiskers was a young woman if someone hadn't told him?

Another important question was *how* Phillip had learned this tidbit of gossip. If Kent broke up with Erin when he met Marian, then it made sense Phillip would have learned this fact after he and Marian divorced. So had Phillip and Marian kept in touch *after* their divorce? Did he hack into her email account, or perhaps know the code to access her voicemails? I had heard stories such things happening with bitter exes.

Also, why had Phillip stayed at Hotel Darlington? Was it more than a coincidence that both Marian and Phillip liked the same place? As small as this town was, it wasn't the only hotel around.

Scanning the expansive lobby, another scenario crept into my mind. Even if Erin had not met Marian until last Thursday, it was possible Marian knew who Erin was, and that she was Kent's ex-girlfriend.

Maybe Marian hadn't been ticked off to find *me* staying at Kent's, but rather to find Erin splash-splashing around in her fiancé's pool. What if Marian had thought Kent had gotten involved once again with Erin?

"Miss?"

I turned back toward the hotel's service desk. The young receptionist was standing next to a woman with gray-black hair pulled into a tight bun at the nape of her neck.

"This is Anna, my manager. She can help with your request." She stepped aside to talk to a guest on the other end of the service desk.

I introduced myself, then held up the photo of Marian and asked as nicely as possible if she had stayed recently at Hotel Darlington.

"I'm sorry, but we do not disclose information on who does or does not stay with us," she said, speaking with an air of authority. "I suggest you go ask this woman yourself."

Rats. This conversation was going nowhere.

Lifting my chin, I mirrored Anna's look of determination. "I understand your policy, but it would be impossible to ask her myself. This woman died recently and it wasn't a natural death."

Anna recoiled, her authoritative demeanor vanishing. "Goodness! I'm sorry to hear—hang on, are you talking about the local woman? The one found this morning in Bonn Creek?"

"Yes, ma'am."

Grimacing, Anna pulled a pair of reading glasses from the front pocket of her burgundy uniform jacket and slid them on, then looked at Marian's photo again. "The poor dear, she's so pretty. Too young to die."

"Do you recognize her as a hotel guest?" I asked again.

Anna took the phone from my hands and swiped two fingers against my screen to zoom in on Marian's face. With a faint gasp, she flicked wide eyes up at me.

Hope surged within me. It was clear Anna recognized Marian from the photo. Now I just needed details on when Marian last stayed here.

"Are you with the police?" she asked.

"No, I'm asking on behalf of her family." It wasn't exactly a lie. Kent was her fiancé—close enough to family—and he would certainly want to bring justice to whoever killed Marian.

"Oh, so you're a private investigator?" she asked.

"Mmmhmm," I squeaked.

Okay, that one was more of a lie.

Anna pressed her lips together, giving Marian's photo one last look. "Well in that case, I can confirm this woman has stayed with us before. Multiple times, in fact."

Bingo. So the bottles of Hotel Darlington hand cream were Marian's. "Did she stay here recently?"

Anna lifted a black wireless phone. "I'm more than happy to help with your investigation, but I feel like I should also share this information with the police. I can call them now, and you can listen to what I tell them. Will that work, dear?"

Uh oh. Time to go. "Actually, I need to get going. Thanks so much for your help."

I breezed through the lobby toward the hotel entrance, where the uniformed doorman held open the door for me. "Enjoy your day, miss."

Footsteps echoed mine as I hightailed it away from the hotel. I looked over my shoulder. The doorman was following me, his brow gathered into a bundle of wrinkles. "Miss? Do you have a minute?"

I stopped walking and waited as he hurried over to me.

"I heard you asking my manager about the woman who was found dead this morning," he said.

"Yes?" I resumed walking toward the opening in the hedges. Was he going to call my bluff on the private investigator fib? Or try to keep me here long enough for Anna to call the cops on me? I didn't think I'd broken any laws by asking questions, but I didn't want to stick around and find out.

The doorman followed me. "Anna hasn't lived in Darlington Hills very long, so she isn't aware that this sorta crime, if that's what it was, never happens around here. I'm afraid the police don't have the experience needed to bring that woman's killer to justice. A private investigator such as yourself is more likely to figure it out."

I recalled Officer Appley, with his trendy side-swept hair, and the way he had suggested I sneak into Kent's upstairs office. I doubted that was a tactic straight from a police academy text-book. Question was, *why* had he made such an unconventional request? Was it inexperience, as the doorman was suggesting, or did he have a habit of bending the rules?

"Did you know Marian Koh?" I asked.

I wasn't usually so blunt, but the doorman seemed willing to talk, and if Anna had called the police, it wouldn't take long for them to arrive.

He glanced back at the hotel as we stepped through the

hedges and onto the street from which I'd come. "I don't know her personally, but I recognized her when I saw her photo in the paper this morning. She's been coming here for the past several months, every two weeks or so."

"Do you know when she stayed here last?"

"Yes, ma'am. It was Thursday—only two nights ago. She walked in shortly before I went home for the evening." The doorman threw a thumb over his shoulder. "She was with the man you were just chatting with in the parking lot, miss. The one with the orange satchel."

Phillip had lied. He'd said he arrived yesterday morning, but according to the doorman, it was actually some time on Thursday. *With Marian.*

He probably figured it didn't matter if he lied to me since I wasn't a cop. But why had he lied? Or was he so upset by Marian's death that he simply misspoke?

My gut told me his relationship with Marian hadn't truly ended with the signing of the divorce papers. What I didn't know was whether their post-marriage relationship was lovey-dovey, or if Phillip had harassed her—or worse—for leaving him?

I thanked the doorman and took off down the street, heading back toward the town square. Unaccustomed to the cruel abuse of high heels, my feet throbbed with each step on the hard pavement. My shoes were leather torture chambers that constricted the life out of my poor toes.

But I was a woman on a mission. First stop was Whisks and Whiskers to ask Erin if she had, in fact, dated Kent. It wasn't likely she had anything to do with Marian's death, but she would probably want to know what Phillip was saying about her.

I kept my eyes ahead, watching for any squad cars heading toward Hotel Darlington. I hoped they were too busy working on the investigation to be bothered with complaints of an out-of-towner asking too many questions.

I slowed my pace. If I called Officer Appley now and filled him in on what I'd learned from the hotel manager, maybe I would preempt any chastisement for impersonating a private investigator.

He'd be so thankful for the info that he'd overlook any rules I may have broken.

I flipped up the front flap of my purse, pulled open the main zipper, then tugged at another zipper inside my bag and felt around for Officer Appley's business card.

My fortress of a purse, though completely on-trend, was as inconvenient as they come. If I got the job at Walnut Ridge, I would buy a new one. I'd had my eye on an oversized Kate Spade tote that would fit my laptop, a project binder, and other typical purse stuff. It was something I could simply stick my hand into and retrieve whatever I needed, rather than navigating obstacles like zippers and magnetic clasps.

My phone rang, and I checked the caller ID. It was Kent.

Abandoning my search for the business card, I answered his call. "Hello?"

"Hadley, this is Kent. Do you have a minute?" His voice was thick with grief.

"Sure. Are you okay? Do you need anything?"

"Actually, that's why I'm calling. I wanted to thank you for all the work you've done so far on my patio, and—"

"The deliveries!" I shrieked. "I meant to cancel the ones I'd scheduled for today, but I completely forgot." I checked the time on my phone's screen. It was a little after 10:30 a.m., which was in the middle of the delivery window for rugs, sun umbrellas, and throw pillows. "Are they there now? If not, I'll call and cancel. I'm sorry, I meant to take care of that earlier this morning."

"No, it's alright. That's not why I'm calling. I wanted to ask if you could finish the project before you fly home."

Say what? He wanted me to finish the project? This weekend?

"Um, sure...if that's what you want," I replied. Maybe he needed a distraction from thinking about Marian?

"Thank you. I had planned to have the new patio ready for Marian's birthday, but now I'll be throwing her one final party, a reception, after her funeral next week. It may sound silly, but I still want everything to be perfect for her, even though she's gone."

"Absolutely. Anything I can do to help, just name it. I'll make sure your outdoor living area is everything she would have wanted it to be." Except for the yellow pool shed, which she had hated. And the yellow umbrellas and throw pillows. It was too late to change those if he wanted everything finalized by the end of the weekend.

"Thanks, Hadley. I appreciate being able to count on you. Can you come over after lunch, say one o'clock or so? I'll handle the delivery crew if they come before you arrive. I'll tell them to put everything off to the side so you can arrange it."

A one o'clock start would give me enough time to go talk to Erin again, grab a sandwich while I was there, and stop by Aunt Deb's to change my clothes and shoes.

I wanted to ask Kent about Phillip, to find out if Marian had ever complained about any sort of harassment by him, but now was not the time. He was grieving, and I didn't want to add to his pain.

"Sure, I'll be there in a couple of hours."

CHAPTER TWELVE

"Marian's ex-husband is a total creep," Erin grumbled when I told her what Phillip had said. "He's the worst of the worst. I can't believe he's gossiping about me. He doesn't even know me." Erin had both hands in her apron pockets. Her disheveled ponytail told me she'd been whizzing around the café all morning.

"But is it true? Did you date Kent?" I kept my voice low, even though there was a good chance no one would hear us. We were standing by the table in the corner where the local animal shelter assisted with cat adoptions. The young man who'd been sitting at the table earlier was on a break. The only ears turned in our direction were pointy ones belonging to the trio of kittens on the nearby play structure.

Erin made a face like she'd eaten something sour. "It was nothing serious. We only went out a few times and then I broke up with him. As it turned out, Kent wasn't my type."

"Not that it matters to me, but Phillip said Kent broke up with you. I'm only telling you because I thought you'd want to know."

"That...*loser*. Who else is he sharing my personal matters with?" Her voice rose enough to turn a few more furry heads in our direction. Though the café was crowded, everyone was busy either talking, eating, or talking while eating.

"I doubt he's told anyone else," I said. "He said he lives in North Carolina, so he probably doesn't know many folks in town."

"I hope you're right, because rumors fly fast around here." She scanned the restaurant as though she were gauging how many customers were already aware of the newest nugget of gossip. "How do you even know Marian's ex-husband? You've only been here a week. It's like you know half the town already."

I considered telling her about Phillip's late-night armed intrusion, but once again, his warning to keep my mouth shut made me do just that. If I decided to tell anyone, it would be the cops.

"It was a chance encounter in town," I replied.

Erin scrunched up her nose. "I don't understand why he would talk about me during your 'chance encounter' with him."

I held up the bag with Aunt Deb's muffin. "He started talking about you and Kent when he saw your logo on this bag."

"What else did he say?" she demanded.

"He said when Kent ended the relationship you didn't handle it well, and—"

"How is one supposed to handle getting dumped?" she snapped.

Erin had a point. I wasn't necessarily handling my breakup well either. Packing and moving to another state definitely was not on the list of ideal methods for coping with a breakup.

"—and Phillip also said you dated Kent and Rhett at the same time." There. It was on the table. As hard as it was to tell her what Phillip had said, I had to do it. It was only right she knew what someone else was saying about her, and I was curious to see how she responded to such accusations.

Erin took a step back until her legs touched the edge of the table for cat adoptions. She sat down. "I started dating Kent and Rhett around the same time," she said. "It wasn't serious with either of them so I didn't feel too guilty about it. Then, I was having dinner with Rhett one evening in Richmond and Kent walked right past our table. He didn't say anything to me; he just gave me one glare that said it all. He was with a group of customers, so he didn't make a scene at the restaurant."

Erin kept her eyes on the door to the café as she spoke. She didn't seem sad or angry. If anything, maybe annoyed.

"Kent didn't say hi to your boyfriend?" I asked. "I thought Rhett worked for Kent."

"Not at that point. The day after Kent saw me on my date with Rhett, he called and broke up with me. Said he was planning to end our relationship anyway because he'd recently met someone else and was planning to take her to Australia."

"Ouch. That would upset me too."

She shook her head. "That's not what made me so upset. Two weeks after Kent broke up with me, Rhett showed up at my café, talking crazy fast like he'd consumed an entire jar of coffee beans, and he told me someone had just hired him away from his current employer, incentivizing him with a salary three times what he was making. Want to guess *who* hired him?"

My jaw fell. "No way...Kent?"

"Yep. He created a new position, Chief Operating Officer, just for Rhett. I was livid. I called Kent and yelled at him, accused him of sabotaging Rhett's career for the sake of revenge. Rhett had already quit his current job when he came and told me about the new one. And I expected Kent to fire him after a week, leaving him with no job whatsoever."

"Did you tell Rhett?" I asked.

Erin cringed. "I should have, but didn't. He'd already quit his job, and if I'd confessed about my relationship—former relationship—with his new boss, then he would've broken up with me and probably turned down Kent's job offer. So Kent and I agreed to never tell anyone that he and I dated. Kent claimed it would make things awkward in the office, and he didn't want that."

"How did Kent get in touch with Rhett? Did the two of them know each other before all of this took place?*"

"No, they'd never met," Erin said. "I don't know how he learned so much about Rhett. Kent has his ways and he knows a lot of people."

"Is Kent a good boss to Rhett?"

"The absolute best, so says Rhett. But I've always felt icky about the situation. You know, like Kent hired Rhett to keep him close, to have some sort of control over his future—our future."

It was hard to imagine Kent doing something so slimy, but maybe his actions were prompted by a broken heart. Although Erin claimed their breakup wasn't a huge deal to her, maybe it had been to Kent.

Erin sighed, sending a gust of air towards the blond tendrils that had come to rest in front of her right eye. "Please don't share this with anyone. Right or wrong, I don't want Rhett finding out, especially now with everything else going on. For the sake of his career and our relationship."

"I promise." Although there was a good chance the police would eventually learn the same information I had.

Erin gave a half-hearted smile. "Thanks. But I don't understand how Phillip knows so much about my relationship history. Kent and I agreed to keep our fling a secret."

"Kent must have told Marian, and then Marian told Phillip. I think the two of them kept in touch after their divorce."

I didn't mention there was a good chance they kept in touch not only figuratively, but also quite literally, if their overnight stay at Hotel Darlington was any indication.

Erin scowled. "Maybe that's why Marian was so awful to us when we were in the pool. Because she knew Kent and I dated."

The sound of a woman's angry voice rose above the chatter in the café, making Erin and me look up. I looked around to pinpoint the source of the voice. It was familiar, and it was not nice.

"Uh-oh. Angry customer," Erin said. She pushed herself off the cat adoption table, stood up straight, and put on a pleasant, how-can-I-be-of-assistance expression.

Peter stood behind the cash register, pointing in our direction. He gave Erin a slight nod, signaling that he was passing the baton to her. As friendly as he was, Peter looked helpless in the face of this angry customer.

The woman turned toward us. Uh-oh was right. It was Celine, Marian's roommate. With her eyes on Erin, she strode toward us, her blonde bob swishing furiously.

"Can I help you, ma'am?" Erin's tone was light and friendly, as though there wasn't a woman coming toward her looking ready to take her down linebacker style.

"Are you the manager?" Celine demanded.

Erin smiled. "I'm the owner. How can I help you?"

"I called an hour ago to place an order for my double espresso iced caramel coffee, and I very clearly said I wanted to pick it up at eleven o'clock. I've been waiting for the last fifteen minutes—" Celine froze, her eyes suddenly shifting to me. "*You.* You're Kent's house guest."

"House *sitter*," I said. "And interior designer. Listen, Celine, I'm so sorry to hear about Marian. I know the two of you were close."

Celine's scowl told me she didn't appreciate my condolences. "Are you still living with Kent?"

I clenched the paper bag holding Aunt Deb's muffin. It didn't matter how many times I told her I wasn't involved romantically with Kent, she wouldn't believe me. "Kent no longer needs someone to look after his house and dog now that he's back in town, so I'm staying with family until I fly home on Monday."

Celine folded her arms. "Do the police know you're leaving town when there's an open murder investigation?"

She was on a tear. There was no reason to continue this conversation with her. The only thing it accomplished, perhaps, was to give her the opportunity to take out her grief on me.

"The detective quoted in this morning's paper didn't confirm it was a homicide," Erin pointed out.

Celine whipped her head toward Erin. "I know what the paper said. I also know Marian had a gunshot wound, and I assure you it was not self-inflicted. Now, as I already mentioned, I would appreciate it if you could give me my double espresso iced caramel coffee, Ms.—" Celine leaned closer, eyeing Erin's name tag—"Ms. Blakely. You need to hire more staff for weekends. This is not acceptable..."

Celine trailed off, her eyes growing wide. "Erin Blakely. I knew your name sounded familiar. Marian told me there's a woman in town who runs a wannabe Starbucks coffeeshop who used to date Kent."

Erin kept her smile on her face. "Starbucks isn't a cat café. And Whisks and Whiskers offers a full menu from 6:30 a.m. until three in the afternoon, with a special brunch selection on weekends."

Celine's face was so red, it looked like she'd run a marathon in the Sahara Desert. "You know what else Marian told me about you? She said you tried to seduce Kent earlier this year."

Erin gasped. "I did not!"

"It was when he had the flu several weeks ago. She said you baked him lasagna and brought it to his house. Marian thought it was rather pathetic you were still chasing after him even though Kent broke up with you."

"What's wrong with being nice?" Erin shot back. "I heard Marian was out of town, and I figured he wouldn't feel like cooking. I may have dated him briefly, but I don't still have feelings for him." A vein bulged on Erin's forehead, becoming more prominent with each word she spoke.

"It's southern hospitality, not *seduction*," I told Celine, though I couldn't help but wonder whether Erin was being completely truthful when she claimed she didn't still have feelings for Kent. It was odd that she had baked him a lasagna. If my ex-boyfriend were to come down with the flu, I wouldn't give him the time of day, much less dinner.

Celine ignored me. Her eyes were now slick with ready-to-fall tears. "It was Marian he loved. Not you."

"I'm well aware of that," Erin snapped. "Hence the marriage proposal."

Celine bristled at Erin's sarcasm. "Then it should have been perfectly clear Kent wasn't interested in you. Or your lasagna." She squeezed her eyes shut, releasing a series of tears. "He was always doing nice things for Marian, like buying her flowers, surprising her with weekend trips to coastal towns. Just last week, he gave her a keychain engraved with her soon-to-be married name, Marian Reading, as an early birthday present. Marian never had any doubt he loved her, so imagine how crushed she must have been when she found another woman staying at his house." A second round of tears flowed as she pinched her eyes closed again.

I recalled the dog keychain that dangled from Marian's fingers when she came into Kent's backyard on Thursday. It was a sweet, albeit misguided gift, considering how little Marian had seemed to care for Chip.

Covering the lower half of her face with her hand, Celine turned on a heel, marched across the restaurant and out the door. Peter ran after her, holding a large Whisks and Whiskers to-go coffee.

"I need to get back to work," Erin said, turning toward the kitchen. "Big crowd today."

"Wait—" I reached out for her arm. "One more question. Did Kent like kangaroos?"

Erin pulled her eyebrows together. "I don't know. Why?"

"I noticed quite a few around his house. On pillows and such." I felt embarrassed asking such a strange question without providing an explanation, but I couldn't admit to sneaking into Kent's upstairs office.

"I don't remember seeing any kangaroos around," she said. "But he was really into cats. Had a small collection of them." Erin pointed toward an orange ceramic cat near the cash register on the coffee bar. "Don't tell Rhett this, but Kent gave that one to me when we were dating. He got it for me because it looks like King Oliver."

It definitely did not look like a cat, much less King Oliver. In fact, it wasn't cute at all. With too-large eyes that bulged past its too-wide nose, it looked like a cross between a troll and Yoda. It would do a better job of scaring away rodents than welcoming customers.

Why would she hang onto such an ugly decoration? Because Kent had given it to her? Or was it because it was a sentimental keepsake?

If so, she wasn't as over Kent as she claimed.

CHAPTER THIRTEEN

When Aunt Deb saw my blistered toes, she presented me with a smorgasbord of bandages and ointments, then insisted I drive her car to Kent's this afternoon.

Five Band-Aids and one quick car trip later, my feet were enjoying their new-found freedom in cushiony flip-flops as I scurried around Kent's pool and patio area, arranging the items that had been delivered earlier today.

Even though the patio umbrellas, with their bright, energetic splashes of yellow, looked amazing next to the cool, soothing tones of the pool, it saddened me to think Marian hadn't wanted yellow accessories in the backyard. She was gone, and now I was decorating her would-be backyard in a color she didn't care for.

But I tried not to think too much about what Marian would or wouldn't have liked. Like Kent, I wanted everything to look perfect for her funeral reception.

After moving all the furniture in the cabana, I unrolled the outdoor rug, centering it in the middle of the space, then repositioned the furniture. I had ordered a rug large enough to place all of the furniture in the sitting area—sectional sofa, coffee table, and swivel chairs—on top of it. One of my frequent reminders to clients was not to skimp on the size of a rug. If it's too small, it can make a room look awkward.

When I was happy with the rug and arrangement of furniture in the cabana, I dug through the big boxes of decorative pillows.

Kent hadn't been kidding when he said he would ask the delivery crew to set everything off to the side. They hadn't even unpacked the boxes.

Not that I minded the work, but I wanted to finish up as soon as possible. Kent was busy receiving a steady stream of visitors offering their condolences. Even though I was mostly in the backyard, I still felt like I was in the way.

Tearing in to a plastic bag containing a striped pillow, I was interrupted by a call from an unidentified number. I pressed the green answer button and put my phone on an unopened box, then switched the call to speakerphone so I could continue unwrapping the pillow.

"Hello?" I said.

"Hi, Miss Hadley, this is Officer Dennis Appley. You have a minute?" His loud, confident voice filled Kent's backyard. I yanked my phone off the box, quickly took it off speakerphone, and brought the phone to my ear.

"Yeah, sure. What's up?" I winced at my word choice, thinking I probably shouldn't answer a call from a cop with 'what's up,' no matter how young he looked.

"Here's what's up: I just got a call from the manager at Hotel Darlington who said she spoke with a private investigator earlier today about Marian Koh's hotel reservation history. She said the P.I. was an attractive young woman with wavy light-brown hair and a small scar on her forehead."

Attractive? I raised my eyebrows, wondering if that was Anna's description or his.

Hopefully his.

"There's gotta be quite a few women in town who fit that description," I said.

"Anna said the P.I.'s name was *Hadley*, Hadley."

I wrinkled my nose, wishing I hadn't told Anna my name.

"She said that?" I asked, my voice an octave higher than usual.

"Yes, and I'm sure you can understand why this surprised me. You know, since you're an out-of-town visitor who has not, in fact, taken the compulsory P.I. training course or obtained a license to be a private investigator, which is required by law in our state."

"She must have misheard me," I countered. "I didn't say I'm a private investigator; I said a private *decorator*. You know, um, for private residences." I bit my lip as I waited for his reply. The last thing I needed was to get in trouble with the cops. Considering how quickly news traveled in Darlington Hills, there was a chance it would further reduce my chances of getting the job at Walnut Ridge.

"Uh-huh, right," he said, his voice filled with playful admonishment. "You better watch yourself, Miss Hadley. If our detective had gotten the call from Anna instead of me, he would've brought you into the station to tell you what I'm telling you now."

"And what exactly are you telling me, Officer?" I asked, surprised by the playful tone of my own voice.

"Leave the investigating to the police. I don't know how they do things in New Orleans, but around here, you need a badge to do police work."

"Don't worry, I'm not trying to be a cop. I'm just curious. I like to ask questions. And I was following up on something I came across while I was staying at Kent's house."

"Oh? And what might that be?"

"I found an overnight bag of Marian's that had a bunch of bottles of hand cream from Hotel Darlington. Which was odd since she lived in this town." Officer Appley was silent, so I continued. "When I stopped by the hotel, I learned that she not only stayed there on multiple occasions, but her most recent stay was with her ex-husband, Phillip Koh."

"Who shared that information with you?" His playful tone was gone. He was now in full-on cop mode.

"The doorman."

"And the doorman volunteered this information to you because...?"

"Because he thought I was a private investigator. He must have misheard me as well."

"Right. Of course. Well then I suggest you start enunciating better," he said, punching out every syllable of his words. "But to be honest, your little white lie has turned us on to a lead in the investigation we had not previously considered."

"Was it a homicide?" I fully expected him to give me the standard 'it's under investigation' response, but it was worth asking. From what I'd learned about Officer Appley so far, he didn't seem to mind bending the rules. Except, apparently, when it came to impersonating a private investigator.

"Yes, it was a homicide. But we haven't officially announced this, so I'll deny telling you if you repeat it to anyone."

"I won't. I promise."

"Anything else?" he asked.

I pressed my lips together, debating on whether I should tell him about Phillip's intrusion last night. His threat to keep my mouth shut still rang in my ears, but now that I knew this was officially a homicide case, I didn't want to withhold any information that could help the police track down Marian's killer.

"There is one thing," I confessed. "Marian's ex-husband came over to Kent's house last night around midnight. He crawled through an unlocked window in the family room. Said he was looking for Marian."

Officer Appley grunted. "You're kidding, right? Because when I took your statement, you didn't mention this. Do you realize withholding information from a police office is a punishable—"

"Phillip threatened me. He said I shouldn't tell anyone if I know what's good for me. Oh, and he had a gun."

"A *gun?*" he bellowed. "Did he point it at you?"

"Not directly. He stuffed it in his pants after a minute or so." I told Officer Appley everything else Phillip had said last night and this morning, including the fact that Chip had seemed oddly comfortable around Phillip.

There was a long, powerful sigh on the other end of the phone. "I'll share this new information with our detective and we will follow up with Phillip. We'll also look into the information you garnered today at the hotel. It's a good lead." But—" his tone turned reproachful again—"do not take that as an invitation to keep asking questions. And steer clear of Phillip. He doesn't have a clean record."

"As in, *police record?*" I yelped. Goosebumps erupted across my arms. I had been alone in a house with an armed man who had a criminal record. "What did he do?"

"It was a domestic dispute when he was in his early twenties with his girlfriend at the time. He was convicted of assault and battery, spent a few months in jail. Maybe he's cleaned up his act since then, maybe he hasn't. That's for us to figure out. No more posing as a P.I., Miss Hadley. Not only does it interfere with our investigation, but it could put you in harm's way. I don't want you getting hurt. Got it?"

"Aye-aye," I said.

"Good. Please just stick to interior decorating and house sitting. Oh, and dog sitting. Have a good day and stay out of trouble."

Rolling my eyes, I said goodbye to Officer Appley and continued unpacking the box of pillows, trying not to think about the scary fact I'd had two run-ins with a convicted criminal. Was Phillip on the police's list of suspects? They must have questioned him already or done some digging into his background. How else would Officer Appley know about his conviction?

I gathered all the plastic wrapping and stuffed it back inside the box, then paused to fan myself with one of the care instruction booklets that came with the pillows. When I'd stopped by Aunt Deb's house earlier, I changed into jeans and a casual three-quarter-sleeve shirt. It wasn't as warm outside as it had been earlier in the week, but it was definitely shorts weather. I was hot and needed some ice water.

I strolled inside through the back door and headed for the kitchen. Kent was standing near his kitchen island talking to a balding man in his forties who was holding an insulated casserole carrier.

"I know you said you already have dinner for tonight," the man said, "so put this one in the freezer and heat it up when you want. My wife stuck a recipe card with re-heating instructions inside the carrier."

"Excuse me," I said as I walked past them. "Just grabbing some ice water." Oh, how I wished I'd brought my own water so I wouldn't have to disturb Kent.

"Hold on, Hadley," Kent said. "I'd like to introduce you to my friend before you go back outside."

Kent's face was shadowed with dark stubble, and his thick hair swirled in every direction but down. He wore a wrinkled white undershirt and jeans with frayed ankle cuffs—not like the trendy type of frayed jeans, but ones that looked like they'd been in his closet since college.

Kent turned to the other man. "Beau, this is Hadley. She's the interior designer I was telling you about whom I hired to redo my outdoor living space for Marian's birthday. She's finishing up this weekend because she heads back home to New Orleans in a couple of days."

I shook Beau's hand. "Hadley Sutton. Nice to meet you."

"Likewise. You must be really good at what you do if Kent flew you in all the way from New Orleans."

I smiled. "Oh, I only met Kent last—"

"I assure you, she's the best designer from here to Louisiana," Kent said. "That's why people pay big bucks for her services."

Big bucks? The project quote I'd given him was on the lower side of average since I wanted to make sure I got the job so I could establish a client base in Darlington Hills in case I got the job at Walnut Ridge.

Kent took a step backwards and walked out of the kitchen. "Speaking of money, I owe you the remainder of your payment. Be right back." He had already paid me half of my fee upfront. It was something I started requiring earlier in my career after a new client refused to pay me when I finished his project.

I opened the cabinet above the three-in-one electric cooker and removed a large plastic cup featuring the Boston Red Sox logo. "Do you and Kent work together?"

"I'm one of his customers," Beau said.

"Do you live in Darlington Hills?"

He shook his head. "I'm about an hour away, in Norfolk. I drove into town today to deliver my wife's lemon chicken casserole." He glanced in the direction where Kent had gone and lowered his voice. "And to offer my condolences, of course."

I filled my cup with ice, then pressed it against the automatic water dispenser on the refrigerator door. "I'm sure he appreciates your kindness."

"Hadley Sutton—with two T's, right?" said Kent, who was scribbling into a checkbook as he padded back into the kitchen.

"That's right," I said.

He tore the check along its perforated edge, then slid it into an envelope. When I finished filling my cup, he handed it to me. "I added a little extra to the price you quoted me for all of your trouble."

"It was no trouble at all, but thank you." I folded the envelope in half and tucked it into the back pocket of my jeans.

Kent gave me a solemn smile. "I couldn't have gotten through the past forty-eight hours without you. I hope you know that." He rolled weary green eyes over to Beau. "You too, man. I couldn't have even made it up to my hotel room Thursday night if it hadn't been for you. No more gin and tonics for me for a while."

Thursday night. The night Marian checked into Hotel Darlington with Phillip.

The last night anyone heard from Marian.

"We've all been there, buddy," Beau said, laughing uncomfortably. "And to be honest, I half-considered feigning my own drunken stupor so I could avoid the rest of that dreadful gala. I can't tell you how many designer dogs they auctioned off while you were passed out upstairs. You had it lucky."

Beau's last word hung in the air, leaving an awkward silence. Wrong word choice. 'Lucky' was the last term anyone should use to describe Kent's situation over the past several days.

Directly behind Beau, sitting on the kitchen countertop next to the microwave, were two new additions to the kitchen: a picture frame holding a photo of Kent and Marian, and a tiny ceramic kangaroo, like the ones I'd seen in the armoire.

My stomach clenched as I imagined the sadness Kent was experiencing. Whether the kangaroo collection was his or Marian's, it was obvious they reminded Kent of her. Probably because Australia was her favorite place, if what Phillip said was true.

"I should get back to work," I said. "Beau, it was nice to meet you."

Chip followed me outside, his fluffy white tail wagging a mile a minute. When I stretched out my hand to pet him, he covered it with slobbery kisses.

"Thanks, sweet boy," I told him as I scratched him behind his ears. "But I can't pet you all day. I have a lot of work left this afternoon and I'm trying to get out of here sooner rather than later."

The back door opened and Kent stepped outside. "I'll be back in a minute," he said to Beau.

He gazed around the pool area, not seeming to focus on

anything. "Things are coming together, I see. You think you'll be able to finish up before you fly home?"

"There's one more delivery tomorrow," I told him. It was all of the smaller outdoor accessories—items that would add another dimension of texture, color, and personality. I had tried to persuade the store to deliver them today, but they didn't have any openings. Fortunately, they agreed to a Sunday delivery. "It's scheduled for ten a.m. tomorrow, so I expect to finish by about noon."

"Wonderful. Thanks." He stared at the new decorative pillow on the sofa, again not seeming to register what he was looking at. "Question for you, Hadley: Since Marian's death is quite possibly a homicide, I want to know if you saw anything out of the ordinary while you were staying here, especially the last couple of nights when she was missing."

Phillip's threat to keep quiet about his late-night intrusion rolled back into my worries, but at this point, I couldn't *not* tell Kent. It was his property on which Phillip had trespassed, and his fiancée someone had killed. My silence was not an option. Besides, I had just told Officer Appley and he would likely contact Kent about it soon.

"Someone did stop by," I said. "Actually, 'stop by' isn't the best way to phrase it, but I think you should know about it. I didn't mention it the other night because I didn't want to upset you even more after the police came over and told you—"

"*Who* came by, Hadley?" His eyes were so intense I felt like they were drilling holes into my mind.

"Marian's ex-husband. I was asleep on the sofa in your family room and he came in through your window. It was unlocked."

"*Phillip* came over? Through my *window*?" he demanded. "How does he even know where I live?"

I shrugged. That was another story; one I didn't particularly want to discuss with Kent. It was probably best if he didn't know Marian was likely still involved with Phillip.

"He didn't hurt you, did he?" His eyes moved across my body as though he were checking for himself.

"No, but he had a pistol."

Kent wrapped his hand around his mouth, muffling an angry growl-like sound.

"He claimed he was looking for Marian. Said some of her coworkers told him she was missing."

"You told the police about this, right?" he asked.

"Yes."

Kent's face was a mess of blotchy red patches and hard lines between his eyes. Not that I'd known him long, but I never would have thought it was possible for someone so elegant, so composed, to look like a man-eating ogre. "Why haven't the police mentioned this to me? Aren't they going to charge him with unlawful entry? *Armed* entry?"

"I'm sure they're working on it," I said. Now wasn't the time to admit I'd reported it to the police less than ten minutes ago.

"Did he take anything?"

"He was here less than five minutes and we talked in the family room the entire time. He was surprised to find another woman staying in your house, but I explained who I am and why I was house sitting. He left through the same window he came in through, carrying only his gun."

"Thank you for telling me," Kent said, sounding slightly calmer. "Now that the police are treating this as a homicide, it is critical you don't withhold any information. From the police or me."

I opened my mouth, ready to tell him about running into Phillip at the hotel, then closed it just as quickly. It was information that would hurt him, which I didn't want to do. Especially not now, when he was already so upset by Marian's death.

"Yes?" he asked. "What else?" Again, his sharp eyes bore into me. "Tell me."

I looked away. He had a right to know, as painful as the truth would be. And there was a chance the police would tell him anyway when they pursued the new lead I'd brought to their attention.

"I ran into Phillip again this morning," I confessed. "He was leaving Hotel Darlington, and from what I understand, he'd been there since Thursday night when he checked in with—"

Nope. Couldn't do it. I couldn't obliterate the happy memories he had of his deceased fiancée.

Kent took a step closer to me. "When he checked in with whom?"

I sucked in a deep breath, which didn't feel like an adequate amount of oxygen to supply my frantically beating heart. "When he checked in with all of his luggage."

"What did he say when you saw him?"

I relaxed a little, relieved he hadn't challenged my lie about the luggage. I wanted to be as honest as possible without disclosing the details about her relationship with Phillip. Especially since I didn't have proof she was still involved romantically with her ex.

"It was a brief conversation," I said. "He was clearly upset about what happened to Marian, and he's hoping the police can make an arrest quickly."

"So he comes into town right before Marian's death—murder, I should say—and then he leaves right after. I trust you told the cops about this conversation as well?"

"Yes. The officer said they'll look into this lead."

"Good. Thank you. I hope you'll continue to answer any of their questions after you fly home."

"Of course."

Kent reached down and lifted the empty box with the plastic pillow wrappings. "I'll take this out to the garage. The recycling truck will pick it up on Monday." He tilted his head and furrowed his brow, seeming to reconsider something. "I'm curious why you were at Hotel Darlington this morning. I thought you were staying with your aunt."

My stomach dropped in the same way it would if I were on a free-falling roller coaster fifty stories high.

If I told him the truth, I would have to tell him about the bottles of hand cream I had found while snooping through his bathroom drawers, which would then lead to questions about why she was staying at the hotel and with whom she was staying.

So the truth was not an option. I needed to tell yet another lie, and I needed to manufacture it at warp speed if I had any hopes of making it believable.

"I was swinging by to say hi to my friend Anna who works there. She's a childhood friend I played with when my family came to town each Christmas. I haven't had a chance to see her this week."

He smiled pleasantly. "I've been keeping you too busy. It would have been a shame if you'd traveled all this way and didn't get to see your friend before you left."

I returned his smile. "Indeed."

Kent pointed to the unopened box of pillows. "I'll let you get back to work. I know you're too busy to stand around and talk to me all day."

He was right. I would be busy praying that, one, Phillip wouldn't find out I'd told both the police and Kent about his late-night intrusion, and, two, that Kent didn't know Anna the hotel manager. Because if he did, he would know that Anna had only recently moved to Darlington Hills.

CHAPTER FOURTEEN

It was 8:30 p.m. by the time I left Kent's house. I could have finished by five o'clock if Kent hadn't gotten a sudden bout of indecisiveness and asked me to rearrange the patio furniture five times.

Instead of driving directly to Aunt Deb's house, I headed for the John Tyler Memorial Highway, which was the closest highway to Darlington Hills. I didn't want Aunt Deb to feel like she needed to cook anything for me this late and there were no fast-food joints in town. There were only sit-down restaurants, which would likely take their time serving me. Speed, it seemed, was not a priority of the local restaurants. I was tired and ready to go to bed.

So I grabbed a cheeseburger at the first fast food place I saw along the highway. It was quick, it was greasy, and it prevented my stomach from imploding. By the time I turned onto Picket Lane, the main road connecting Darlington Hills to the highway, I had already finished my burger and half my lemonade.

Picket Lane was a long, narrow road elevated on a manmade embankment since it crossed several low-lying areas that flooded easily. Darlington oak trees lined the road on both sides. Their branches twined overhead, forming a tunnel-like enclosure for nearly a mile.

During the day, Picket Lane was enchanting. It was my favorite road in the country, and one I could spend all day winding up and down with my music turned up and windows rolled down.

At night, it was nothing short of spooky. There were more shadows than light, and the area on either side of the embankment was a dark abyss. The historic-looking street lamps along the road, while charming, did little to improve visibility.

I turned on my brights and pressed my foot against the gas pedal, driving slightly over the speed limit. If I'd been in my own car, I would have driven faster. But I didn't want to get pulled over for speeding in Aunt Deb's car since I wasn't on her insurance.

Yawning, I lifted my lemonade from the cupholder next to me and brought the straw to my lips, hoping the cold, sugary drink would help keep me alert. Only five more minutes and then I'd be pulling into Aunt Deb's driveway. Until then, I needed to stay awake.

It had been a long afternoon. Kent, who had initially given me almost complete control over all design choices, suddenly became very particular about what he wanted. Although he was apologetic about it, he asked me to essentially redo everything I'd done thus far. After trying every possible arrangement of furniture, he finally decided he liked it exactly how it was before we started moving everything around.

Often times, clients didn't know what they did or didn't like until they saw it for themselves. And under normal circumstances, I involved them more in the furniture and decor selection process.

But nothing about this situation was normal.

I understood why Kent wanted everything to be perfect, so I patiently tried most of his suggestions, disagreeing with only the most absurd arrangements. And Kent was a paying client, so I wanted him to be pleased with the end result.

I was thankful to have my first project—and client reference —in Darlington Hills in case I got the job and moved here. I'd almost felt bad about accepting the second half of Kent's payment today considering everything he was going through.

Remembering that Kent had said he 'added a little something extra' to my check, I returned the lemonade to the cup holder and removed the folded envelope from the back pocket of my jeans. I hadn't wanted to open the envelope when he gave it to me; it wouldn't have been polite to do so in front of his customer. Then I forgot about it during the busy afternoon.

Keeping my eyes on the road, I placed the envelope in my lap. He hadn't licked it, so I lifted the flap easily, removed the check, and glanced down at it.

I nearly swerved into the other lane when I saw the amount. One thousand extra dollars. *What?* In what universe was a thousand dollars 'a little something' extra? This was huge. If I got the job, it would help with my moving expenses. And now I could definitely buy the Kate Spade tote to replace the many-zippered fortress of a handbag I was carrying around now. I needed something cute but practical, and one that wasn't inspired by the Alcatraz prison system.

I looked at the check again to make sure I'd read it right. Yep, one thousand dollars over what he owed me. One thousand extra from the very generous Kent Reading—

Uh-oh. He had forgotten to sign it.

I squeezed the steering wheel, feeling frustrated. It had been an oversight, right? He wouldn't intentionally leave off his signature, would he? Or was it his way of making sure I came back tomorrow to finish the job?

Either way, I felt uneasy about it.

Placing the check on the passenger seat, I returned my full attention to the road. Bright lights from a vehicle behind me reflected off my rearview mirror, making me squint. Didn't they see me ahead of them? Why weren't they turning off their brights? I reached up to the rearview mirror, feeling for the lever that would dim the reflection.

I found it, flipped it, then checked the rearview mirror again. The hazy, dimmed reflection told me the car behind me was much closer than before. And it was going very fast. Now it was on my left, getting ready to pass me on the narrow two-lane road.

I tapped the brake pedal to allow the other car to pass me. There was a brief screech of tires and then a thunderous crash as the car rammed into my front left fender, propelling me toward the narrow shoulder on the road.

Something splattered across my chest and leg.

I screamed. Was it blood? Was I hurt?

Braking hard, I forced the steering wheel to the left so I wouldn't fly off the road and down the embankment.

I swerved into the oncoming lane, then pulled the wheel to the right to avoid jumping the embankment on the opposite side. Only after I had regained control of the car and slowed down did I realize the wet stuff that drenched me was my lemonade, which had flown from the cupholder.

Where was the other car? Had it gone over the side of the embankment?

Headlights in my left sideview mirror told me it was still in the oncoming lane, slightly behind me. This time I sped up.

I'd been in a fender-bender once before in New Orleans, and both the other driver and I had pulled over and exchanged insurance information. But it had been in the middle of the day on a road with a wide shoulder that made pulling over safe.

This time, I didn't know where to pull over to swap insurance details. Or even if I should stop at all. What had caused the other car to lose control and ram into me? An animal on the road?

If that were the case, why was the other car still on the wrong side of the road? Clearly, the driver was not in control of their car. They were probably either asleep at the wheel or intoxicated.

I need to call the police. Reaching for my handbag, I pulled on the top zipper, but it got stuck when it was halfway open. I tugged again, feeling a mounting urge to find my phone and dial 9-1-1. Something was wrong.

Picket Lane veered to the left. I was approaching one of the sharper curves on this stretch of the winding road. I slowed slightly, keeping my eyes on all my mirrors. The other car was still in the oncoming lane, only it wasn't slowing down.

Veering left along the curve, I braked hard as the other car attempted once again to pass on my left.

"Don't pass on the curve!" I yelled as if they could hear me. They were now in front of me, and I got a two-second look at its license plate before its brake lights lit up and the car slowed.

It was now driving alongside me, mirroring my speed. The car was black, its driver a shadow hidden by tinted windows.

The car swerved left, then plowed into me a second time. I tried to force the steering wheel to the left, but my momentum toward the embankment was too much.

As my tires neared the edge of the road, I impulsively pulled the steering wheel to the right in hopes of driving down the slope instead of rolling down it side over side.

I screamed all the way down the embankment, braking hard and clenching the steering wheel. My headlights illuminated the wide trunk of a tree directly in front of me seconds before I crashed into it.

CHAPTER FIFTEEN

Someone's trying to kill me. Up there, on the embankment. Trying to kill me.

Instinct told me to run. Shoving the airbag out of the way, I unfastened my seatbelt and reached for my purse in the passenger seat.

It wasn't there. Had someone taken it?

No, not possible. I looked out my window, expecting to see the black car pummeling toward me down the embankment. But the only movement above came from a pair of red taillights speeding away along Picket Drive.

Must get out of the car.

I checked the passenger seat again, confused. My purse was here a moment ago, now it was gone.

I couldn't worry about my purse. I had to get out. Pulling on the handle, I shoved open the door, making the interior lights come on.

One foot out of the car, I stopped, catching a glimpse of my purse on the floorboard of the passenger seat. I dove for it, then scurried away as quickly as possible, running toward the safety of darkness among the trees.

I'd forgotten to turn off the car, so the interior lights and headlights shined like a beacon. I considered going back to turn off the lights so whoever had sideswiped me wouldn't easily spot it, but I didn't want to take that chance in case the driver was already down in the woods looking for me.

I ran until I found a wide patch of shadows near some trees and a wooden post-and-rail fence. I sank onto the grass and listened.

There was no road noise and no sounds from whatever night-time critters lived in these woods. Not even a whistle of wind. Even the tiniest of creatures had paused their busy lives to watch the mayhem unfolding below. Either that, or they were in as much of a state of shock as I was.

Every fiber of my body shook violently, but nothing hurt. I stretched out my arms and legs to check anyway. No blood, not even a scratch.

Setting my purse on the grass in front of me, I wrestled with the zipper until it gave way, then fished out my phone and called the police.

I waited in the dark by the fence until the trees lit up with red and blue swirling lights, exactly eight minutes later. A patrol car stopped along the side, a little further down from where I was.

An officer stepped out of the car and shined a flashlight down the side of the embankment. When the beam of light rolled across Aunt Deb's car, the officer walked toward it.

Joining the policewoman at the front of the car, I cringed when I saw the crumpled hood and shattered headlights.

The officer, a middle-aged woman with a plain and tidy updo, tsk-tsked her way around the permitter of Aunt Deb's car. "You think this is bad, you should see what vehicles look like after they crash while driving over forty miles per hour. You're lucky you weren't going any faster when you struck the tree."

I didn't want to imagine what would have happened if I hadn't braked at the last minute. I'd save that nightmarish visualization for another time, if ever.

She held out a badge. "Officer Patty Carmen. And you are?"

"Hadley Sutton," I said, struggling to find my voice.

"Are you hurt, hon? Need any medical attention?"

I reassured Officer Carmen I was fine, then gave a nonsensical account of everything that happened, from the point when I first noticed the car's headlights until I crashed into the tree and saw taillights zipping along Picket Lane toward Darlington Hills.

"Did you notice any cars traveling back down this road, toward the highway, after you crashed into the tree?"

"No. Yours was the first car I've seen since the other one drove away."

Pressing her lips together, she nodded like I'd said something interesting. "Did you by chance catch the car's make and model? License plate number?" She flipped open a spiral notebook and pulled a pen from her pocket.

"It was a black car, I think. I don't know the model, but it was smallish."

"Two door or four doors?"

"Um…"

She pointed to Aunt Deb's car. "Bigger or smaller than this one?"

"About the same." Aunt Deb's was a four-door sedan, around two years old.

"License plate?"

"I only caught the last letter. It was a D. Or maybe an O. Or…"

Officer Carmen stopped writing and looked up from her notepad.

"I guess it could have been a zero." I pressed my fingertips against my eyes. "Sorry, I know that's not going to help you much."

"Actually, it might," she said matter-of-factly. "Now here's the

113

important question: do you have any idea who would do this to you? Have you had any disagreements recently with anyone?"

"You might want to talk to Officer Appley," I told her. "Earlier today I was asking around about Marian Koh, the woman found in Bonn Creek last night. I think my questions struck a hot nerve with someone."

CHAPTER SIXTEEN

"Look at these snapdragons!" Aunt Deb pinched the stem of one and brought it to her nose. "Can you imagine seeing these beauties every morning on your way to work?"

"They are pretty," I agreed. "And it's not even officially spring yet. Imagine this garden in a month or so."

Aunt Deb nodded emphatically. Bringing her hand in front of her face to hide a yawn, she scanned the picnic area to the right of the apartment complex's flower garden. "My, oh my, would you look at those barbecue grills over there. I see one, two...*three* grills out here. Wow. That's more than the first complex we toured. They're so... um, clean, as far as grills go. This community obviously has very considerate residents who tidy up after themselves." She nodded as though agreeing with herself.

"Aunt Deb—"

"Imagine cooking burgers out here on a Saturday evening with a pitcher of iced tea. Wouldn't it be lovely?"

I was apartment hunting with Aunt Deb, not because I thought I would get the job, but because she wanted me to. Considering that her car looked like a busted piñata, I was happy to go along with anything she wanted. Even though it was quite possibly a waste of time considering how well my interview went.

I held back a smile. "They *are* the cleanest grills I've ever seen. Probably because no one uses them." I nudged her arm playfully with my elbow. As hard as Aunt Deb was trying to promote this complex, she might as well have been the leasing agent.

"You don't need to convince me to move to Darlington Hills," I told her. "One homicidal maniac isn't going to scare me away. I'd rather dodge the loonies around here than live in the same town as my ex."

"Really? After everything that's gone on the past couple of days, I figured you'd skedaddle as soon as the sun rose this morning and never look back."

I wrapped my arms around Aunt Deb's narrow shoulders and gave her a hug. "Nope, this is where I want to be. I just need to get the job, which I'm not so sure is going to happen."

She pulled away and leveled her eyes at mine. "Don't you start convincing yourself you didn't get the job. That man has built quite the home furnishings empire, and he didn't get there by being a dummy. He won't pass on a talented designer such as yourself because you couldn't solve his cockamamie math riddle."

"Thanks. I hope you're right."

Aunt Deb's long-sleeve cotton blouse, adorned with floral embroidery and scalloped edges, fluttered and billowed in the morning breeze. She pointed to the swimming pool. "Shall we carry on?" Her voice was chipper, but her frequent yawns and puffy eyes told me she was as exhausted as I was.

Aunt Deb began most days at seven a.m. with enough energy to jumpstart an eighteen-wheeler. Today, she looked more like an eighteen-wheeler had run over her.

As did I. Neither one of us got much sleep last night after what happened on Picket Lane. Aunt Deb wasn't upset about her car, so she claimed, but was livid that someone would try to hurt me. If her car hadn't been towed to a local body shop, she likely would have driven around all day looking for the mystery black car. I would have joined her because I was just as furious someone would ram into me and smash Aunt Deb's car.

The tow truck driver said her car was beyond repair, which meant she'd have to buy a new one with money I knew she didn't have right now. Darlington Mini Storage had fewer customers in recent months due to maintenance and security issues that were beyond her budget to fix.

Around midnight, after three cups of lemon ginger tea at Aunt Deb's kitchen table, both of us had stopped shaking and started yawing. It took me two hours after that to fall asleep, and I slept in until seven o'clock, when I awoke from a dream that I was driving over the side of a highway, plummeting to my death, while being chased by a flying Godzilla. It was a lovely way to start the day.

I turned toward the pool gate. "Sure, let's keep exploring. So far, I like this complex better than the other." We were at the Wooded Oaks Apartments, which was a five-minute walk to Aunt Deb's and ten minutes to the Walnut Ridge home.

Before we toured Wooded Oaks, Aunt Deb took me to a complex across the street from her home, but the grounds weren't well maintained and the units seemed much older. I opened the gate of the cast iron fence bordering the pool and we stepped onto the pool decking. It made me think of Kent's pool, even though it wasn't as luxurious. I would enjoy floating in it nonetheless.

My phone rang. I removed it from the back pocket of my jeans, checked the caller ID, then promptly stuffed it back into my pocket.

"You're not going to answer that?" Aunt Deb looked appalled, as though I were committing an abominable social sin.

"Nope. It's the police."

Her jaw went slack. "All the more reason to answer it. Maybe they have information about who ran you off the road last night."

"I doubt it. It's the officer I spoke with yesterday who warned me against going around town asking questions about Marian. He told me it could put me in harm's way. Unfortunately, he was right. Now he's probably calling to dole out a great big 'I told you so.' I'm not in the mood for that right now, so I'll call him back later." To avoid any temptation to answer his call, I transferred my phone from my pocket to the deep, dark abyss of my purse.

"Who were you talking to about Marian?" she asked.

"Pretty much everyone I've met so far in Darlington Hills."

"Oh! My goodness, hon. You sure do like to talk, don't you? You'll fit right into this town." Aunt Deb ducked her head and gazed stealthily around the pool area. "Just be careful, would you?" she whispered. "Talk all you want, but not about Marian. Someone around here doesn't like you getting involved in this."

"But *who?*" I mused. "And why? Because I know something I shouldn't about Marian?"

"I don't know. Has anyone around here made you feel uneasy?"

"Um…" I paused, considering whether I should tell her about Phillip's armed intrusion. It would likely send her into a fit of anxiety. She had lived in Darlington Hills since marrying my uncle, and I didn't want to destroy whatever sense of security she felt. Especially now that Uncle Bill was gone and she lived alone.

"Go on, spit it out. Who rattled you? I might have to tell them off for spooking you."

"It was Marian's ex-husband, but don't even think about talking to him. If you're unfortunate enough to ever meet the man, run in the other direction."

"What'd he say?"

"You don't want to know. Might give you nightmares."

She swished a hand at me. "Pfft. I watch R-rated movies— ones with car chases and such. I can handle a good dose of drama every now and then."

I recounted the story of Phillip's late-night visit and our subsequent conversation in the Hotel Darlington parking lot.

Aunt Deb put her palms together under her chin as though she were gearing up for a prayer. "Please tell me you told the police about this."

"I did, even though Phillip warned me not to. He said if I know what's good for me, I'd keep my mouth shut. Sounds rather ominous, doesn't it?"

Aunt Deb bowed her head and moved her lips in a silent prayer.

"It's possible Phillip found out I told Kent and the police about his intrusion," I said. "Maybe one of them confronted him about it yesterday." It was logical they would.

"Do you think Phillip killed Marian?" Aunt Deb asked.

I shrugged. "I don't know. I found out yesterday he spent some time in jail when he was in his twenties for hurting his then-girlfriend."

"Once a hitter, always a hitter," Aunt Deb said. "If he hurt a woman badly enough to get jail time, I'd imagine he might do it again—or worse."

"Only thing is, when I saw him at the hotel, he seemed genuinely saddened by her death."

She pressed her lips together and considered this. "Does Phillip have a black car, like the one that ran you off the road?"

"The car Phillip had in the hotel parking lot was a silver sedan, but Erin—" I closed my mouth, not wanting to voice the worry that had been plaguing me all morning.

"What?" she pressed.

I sighed, feeling guilty to even bring it up. "Erin, the owner of Whisks and Whiskers, has a black Honda. She drove it to Kent's house the day she came over to swim. And then I found out yesterday—from Phillip—that she dated Kent before he got involved with Marian."

Aunt Deb's lips puckered into an O-shape. "Does Erin know Phillip told you all this?"

"Yes, I asked her about it yesterday. She claimed she wasn't too upset when Kent broke up with her, but then I learned she recently made him lasagna when he was ill."

Aunt Deb nodded knowingly. "Sounds like she still has feelings for Kent."

"I suspect she does. The first time Erin met Marian was when we were floating in Kent's pool, and she was quite rude to Marian. Erin left in a huff because Marian had told us to get out of the pool."

"She could have been jealous of Marian," Aunt Deb said.

"Right, and can you believe that the creepy-looking cat figurine by Erin's cash register was a gift from Kent? He gave it to her when they dated. Makes me think it's sentimental."

"Oh! That dreadful thing gives me the heebie-jeebies every time I look at it. But I don't know...Erin seems like such a sweet girl. She wouldn't have run you off the road."

"Erin doesn't want the word to spread about her relationship with Kent." I lowered my voice. "Especially since she hasn't told her boyfriend, who happens to work for Kent."

Feeling too lazy to dig through my purse for my phone, I glanced at Aunt Deb's watch to check the time. If I left the Wooded Oaks complex in the next twenty minutes, I'd have time to walk by Whisks and Whiskers on my way to Kent's house to check the parking lot in the back. Just to make sure Erin's car didn't have any large dents on the right side. It wouldn't be much of a detour, and I had my sneakers on today.

"Just don't tell your parents about any of this," Aunt Deb said. "They'll forbid you from ever moving here."

I laughed. "Thankfully, I'm no longer twelve and I can make my own decisions."

A cheerful ringtone sounded behind us. A young woman carrying a large paper grocery sack in her arms was fishing through her purse with her free hand. She removed her phone, but her purse strap slid down her shoulder. As she dashed to retrieve it, several apples rolled out from the top of the grocery sack, followed by half a dozen plums.

I headed toward the woman, collecting rogue apples and plums on my way over. Aunt Deb followed, catching a few more stragglers.

"I hope you have a liberal interpretation of the five-second rule," I said, returning the fruit to the top of her sack.

"If there's one thing I don't worry about, it's germs," she said. "I'm the principal at Darlington Hills Middle School, which I'm convinced is the epicenter of all germs in North America." Laughing, the woman put her phone into the grocery sack and held out her hand. "I'm Carmella. Did you just move in?"

"Hadley Sutton," I said, shaking her hand. "I'm looking at apartments because I hope to move here soon. The leasing office was closed, so my aunt and I are taking it upon ourselves to tour the complex—or trespass, depending on how you look at it."

"I'm no leasing agent, but if you have any questions, please ask away." Carmella introduced herself to Aunt Deb and graciously received the two apples she had picked up.

Carmella was tall, black, with a sleek bob that framed her angular jawline. She wore emerald green yoga pants and, despite the morning's cool breeze, a white sleeveless tank top that showed off arms so toned I felt inspired to start lifting weights or doing pushups. She looked to be about my age, somewhere in her early thirties. And though she wasn't wearing much makeup, she had long, wispy eyelashes that I could only assume were artificial. Either that, or she was a direct descendant of a beauty goddess.

Carmella's phone rang inside the paper sack.

"Don't let us keep you from answering your phone," Aunt Deb said.

"It's my boyfriend, I'll call him back. I've been waiting on him to propose for the past five years; he can wait on me for five minutes."

Aunt Deb's light blue eyes ignited with purpose and ambition. I was familiar with this look. It was the one she wore anytime the topic of men, marriage, or babies arose, which seemed to occur more frequently in the last several years. "Well dear, maybe that's why he's calling—to propose to you."

"If he's proposing to me over the phone, I'm saying no," she deadpanned. "He's gonna have to hop on a plane and ask me in person if he wants me to say yes. Preferably on one knee."

Setting down the grocery sack, she dug through her purse again, this time retrieving a key. "I don't know how many units are available at Wooded Oaks, but there's a one-bedroom directly below me that's empty right now. Would you like me to show you inside my apartment? It's the same floor plan. I can't promise it's the tidiest it's ever been, but it'll give you an idea of what the units are like here."

We happily took up her on her offer and toured her apartment. Not only did I love the layout and size, I also enjoyed getting to know Carmella and I became excited at the possibility of being her neighbor.

On my way out, I studied her front door. "I love your wreath," I said, admiring the vivid red and yellow tulips. "Did you buy it in town?" If I did move to Darlington Hills, I needed to know which stores sold decorations as nice as this one.

She tugged on a bow to straighten it. "No, I made it. I'm ready for springtime even if it isn't ready for me."

"Wow, it's beautiful," I said. "Do you sell them?"

"Actually, I do. I make a bunch every year for the Flower Festival, which is held in April. Proceeds go to the local animal shelter."

Aunt Deb studied the wreath. "You already have one customer for this year's event. I'll be sure to stop by your table."

"Thanks!" Carmella said, beaming.

To the right of Carmella's front door was a white box featuring a bell symbol that said 'push' and a glass circle that looked like the lens of a camera. I pointed to it. "Nice doorbell. Looks like a good security feature."

"It didn't come with the apartment," Carmella said. "I installed it after I moved in because I live by myself and I'm a worrier with a capital w. It has a camera that starts recording when someone comes to the door." She faced the camera and waved. "But it was easy enough to install. Only took me fifteen minutes, and the apartment's management board didn't have an issue with it, as long as I promised to leave it here whenever I move out."

Security camera. By the front door. My mind spun with new questions. Did Kent have one in the front of his house? I didn't recall seeing one, but maybe it was in a more obscure location than Carmella's.

If Kent did have one out front, was that why Phillip had come in through a window in the *back?* It couldn't have been a coincidence that he had found an unlocked window. He must have known exactly where and how to get in. Not only that, but someone—Marian, I presumed—must have kept the window unlocked for him. He'd had an open invitation to come inside.

As I approached Whisks and Whiskers, the scent of buttery pastries and coffee grew thicker. It took every ounce of willpower to not stop at my new favorite café. It was best to avoid Erin until I got a good look at her car and make sure she wasn't the one who sideswiped me.

I turned right, following the side street alongside the café, then cut left into the parking lot behind Whisks and Whiskers. If Erin saw me snooping around the lot, I'd have to come up with an excuse fast. Maybe I'd say something along the lines of wanting to get in some extra steps before going to Kent's. It wasn't entirely untrue.

As expected, the parking lot was packed. Last Sunday when I'd come here for brunch with Aunt Deb, we had to wait twenty minutes for a table. Whisks and Whiskers was a popular hangout for the after-church crowd, and judging from the parking lot, today's brunch crowd appeared to be just as big.

There were roughly twenty cars parked behind the café. I circled the lot, not only looking for Erin's black Honda, but also inspecting the right sides of several other black mid-sized cars.

Erin's car was not in the parking lot.

My body stiffened. Why wouldn't she be at work? Sunday was her busiest day and she was short-staffed as it was. I supposed Erin could be sick, but she seemed fine yesterday when I spoke with her. And I doubted she walked to work because she lived in the newer section of Darlington Hills, closer to the highway, which would be a little far to walk.

Or, perhaps she was working, but didn't drive today. Maybe because something was wrong with her car—like banged up driver's-side doors?

The back door to the café opened and three small children spilled into the parking lot, chased by parents yelling at them to slow down. I eyed the exit to the lot and then the café's back door.

Was Erin inside Whisks and Whiskers? It would be easy enough to check, but I told Kent I'd arrive by eleven and it was already 11:15 a.m. Aunt Deb and I had stayed at Wooded Oaks longer than I intended, but I'd enjoyed talking with Carmella so much that time got away from me.

I gave the back door one last glance, then turned toward the street and headed for Kent's. Now wasn't the time to track down Erin's whereabouts. I'd work diligently to finish the patio area in two to three hours, then swing by Whisks and Whiskers afterwards to get a late lunch and see if Erin was inside.

Thin, wispy clouds spread their feathery tendrils across the sky, promising a day of sunshine. This was my last full day in Darlington Hills and I wanted to enjoy it as much as possible since I didn't know when I would return. It could be as soon as several weeks if I were lucky enough to get the job, or as late as Christmas, when my parents would fly in from Japan and we would all stay at Aunt Deb's house.

The thought of having to wait until the end of the year to return made my stomach feel hollow. I had always loved this town, but after flirting with the idea of calling it my own, I grew even more attached to it. I'd found an apartment I liked, acquired a local client, become familiar with some of the nearby home decor suppliers and contractors, and even met a couple of friends.

I'd also made an enemy.

After what happened last night, it was clear I was making someone nervous. I was on the right track; I just didn't know which was the right one. Erin had the same type of car as the one that hit me last night, but she wasn't the only one I'd talked to about Marian's death. I'd also spoken with Phillip, Kent, Celine, Anna at the hotel, and Officer Appley. Any of them could have then relayed our conversation to others, and word could have spread quickly that I was asking questions about Marian.

As I crossed the town square towards Kent's neighborhood, I considered my recent conversations about Marian. Yesterday I told Kent about Phillip's late-night intrusion. The news had upset him, but his anger didn't seem directed at me.

If Kent had known Marian was still involved with Phillip, he could have been angry enough to kill her. But he had been out of town, and his customer had confirmed this fact yesterday. Could he have hired a hitman?

It didn't seem likely. I doubted Darlington Hills, one of the friendliest towns in the nation, had a thriving black market of hitmen.

Celine was also upset yesterday, but more so at Erin than me. From what I'd learned, Marian and Celine had a rocky relationship and had gotten into a number of arguments. But that didn't mean Celine would kill Marian. Celine had been so concerned about Marian the evening she didn't return home—enough to come knocking on Kent's door in the middle of the night.

Aside from the question of *who* tried to kill me last night on Picket Lane, another unsettling question remained: how long had they been following me before they sideswiped me? It was dark by the time I'd left Kent's house, so it seemed like I would have noticed if taillights had shone in my rearview mirror all the way from Kent's to the burger joint to Picket Lane.

Or, maybe not. I'd been so tired, I probably wouldn't have noticed someone sitting in the back seat of Aunt Deb's car until they reached out and grabbed me.

I approached Kent's two-story brick home, but instead of taking the driveway leading to his backyard, I walked half a dozen more steps and turned onto the paved walkway to the front of his house. I studied his doorbell. There was no box with a security camera like the one by Carmella's door. His looked like a regular one-push, ding-dong type of bell. Nothing fancy.

At his doorstep, I gave his porch a 360-degree scan. Kent didn't have one security camera. He had two, both perched above his door at different angles.

If Carmella, a self-proclaimed 'worrier with a capital w,' had *one* security camera, what did that make Kent?

CHAPTER SEVENTEEN

As much as I had always loved the traditional, southern style of interior design, I also adored vibrant, whimsical bohemian patterns for accent pieces like plates, serving bowls, and decorative pillows.

Such was the style of the dinnerware I'd selected for Kent's patio. Decorated with botanical and geometric designs in hues of pale yellow, faded teal, and earthy reds, the plates added sophisticated dashes of color to the otherwise neutral place settings.

I reached into one of the six boxes delivered earlier today and removed another dinner plate, then set it on the oval patio table, which was large enough to seat twelve. Kent had asked me to set the table for Marian's funeral reception before I left.

I set a smaller, coordinating salad plate on top of the dinner plate, then slid a woven hyacinth plate charger under them both to add another layer of texture and style.

My heart ached for Kent and whomever else would be eating from these plates while mourning Marian's death. In reality, it didn't matter how stylish or beautiful the place setting was. Nothing would change the miserable reason why Kent's guests would be eating from them later this week.

His patio project was nearly complete. I'd finished arranging all of the other decorations that arrived, placing ceramic garden stools next to swivel chairs and topping them with woven drink coasters that matched the plate chargers. A crew had just left after delivering and hanging a bronze cast-aluminum curtain rod and white outdoor curtains on the west side of the cabana, which would minimize the heat from the late-afternoon sun.

Everything was done except for the place settings. I'd completed seven and had about fifteen more to go at the various seats around the backyard.

It was 12:30 p.m. and my stomach was hating me for not grabbing a to-go lunch from Whisks and Whiskers when I swung by the parking lot earlier. It didn't help that I was laying out the plates, imagining all the food that would soon fill them.

I had already asked Kent to sign my check, which he did after apologizing profusely, so I planned to leave as soon as I finished the place settings and received the final thumbs-up from him. Then I would go by Erin's café one more time.

If she was there, but her car wasn't, I'd tell her about what happened to me last night and watch her reaction. She had been a jittery mess yesterday, and I wondered what sort of mood she was in today.

"Hey, Hadley, I'm leaving to pick up a sandwich," Kent called from the back door. "Can I get something for you?"

Hallelujah. My stomach wouldn't implode after all. "Thanks! I'd love a turkey and cheese on wheat."

Less than a minute after his truck roared down the street, I took a break from setting the table and went into his kitchen to refill my glass of water.

As iced cubes clinked their way down the refrigerator's automatic dispenser and into my glass, my eyes fell on the kangaroo figurine sitting next to the framed photo of Kent and Marian. Were the kangaroos in the upstairs office his collection or Marian's? Did he keep that room locked out of embarrassment, or was there something else in there he didn't want anyone to see?

I hadn't seen anything in there that looked particularly valuable; just a bunch of Australian and African safari decor, photos and the odd collection of kangaroos. Had I missed something? I needed to look again. This was my last chance to find out what in the world Kent wanted to keep hidden up there.

I looked out the kitchen window and down the street. Wherever Kent had gone to get sandwiches, it would take at least fifteen minutes. Probably more since most restaurants would be busy with lunchtime crowds.

Leaving the kitchen, I hustled though the back door to the swivel chair in the cabana where I'd left my handbag. I had haphazardly thrown Marian's hairpin in there Friday night after I locked Kent's office, not because I thought I might return but because I didn't want to trespass into his bathroom again just to return it to Marian's drawer.

In a record-breaking fifteen seconds, I unzipped my way through my bag's labyrinth of pockets and found the hairpin. As I slid my hand out of my bag, my fingers brushed against an unfamiliar object. It was long and cylindrical with a pointy tip.

A pen?

I frowned. There were countless times I'd wished I had a pen in my bag but didn't, but this was the first time I found a pen in there that wasn't mine.

I pulled it out of my bag and read the inscription on the side. Hotel Darlington.

What? How had this ended up in my bag? I slid it in the back pocket of my jeans and went back inside, heading for the stairs. Now wasn't the time to retrace my steps and try to solve that mystery.

Chip looked up from his sherpa dog bed at the foot of the stairs, wagged his tail for a short measure, then curled into a ball and closed his eyes. I was thankful he didn't follow me.

I slid the hairpin into the door's handle exactly as I had done Friday night.

Click. In one swift motion, I pulled on the handle and opened the door. I reached for the light switch, then froze.

The lights were already on. Kent had been in the room recently.

I glanced in the closet, then opened the armoire. Now there were two missing kangaroos, Mary Lou and Brandie, according to the nameplates. All the other kangaroos were in place as far as I could tell.

Next I headed for the small table by the window. There was nothing on top, but it seemed dustier than two days ago. Lowering one knee to the floor, I peered inside the trash can. It still held the same broken kangaroo. I removed the two halves from the bin and turned them in the palm of my hand, inspecting them.

I flinched. Tiny holes were drilled through the eyes, making it look like a soul-sucking beast from a horror movie. Another hole was drilled through the bottom side of the kangaroo next to a Made in China sticker. This hole had a slightly larger diameter than the ones through the eyes.

So strange. Why had he drilled holes into the kangaroo?

The back of my neck prickled as I shifted my gaze between the bottom half of the kangaroo and the thick layer of dust on the table. Why was he mutilating the kangaroos? Was it some sort of sick compulsion, or maybe a voodoo ritual that involved a drill instead of needles, and kangaroos instead of dolls? I'd occasionally seen voodoo dolls in shops in New Orleans, but ceramic kangaroo mutilation was new to me.

I recalled the kangaroo Kent had recently placed in his kitchen. Was that Mary Lou? Or maybe Brandie, the most recent kangaroo to go missing from the armoire?

What troubled me more than the kangaroo collection or the holes through their eyes was that they all had female names.

It was time to leave this room, race to finish setting the tables, and then leave.

But first, I had to get some photos for Officer Appley. I retrieved my phone from my pocket, snapped a photo of the mutilated kangaroo and then the collection inside the armoire. After returning everything in the room to its original place, I locked the door behind me.

On my way down the stairs, I texted the photos to the same number Officer Appley had used when he tried calling me earlier this morning. I hoped it was his mobile number, since he wouldn't be able to receive my text via a landline.

HADLEY

Thought you might want to see these photos. I had to borrow a stapler again.

I trusted he would understand the stapler euphemism was code for going into Kent's office. Hopefully he wouldn't give me a hard time about snooping since it had been his idea in the first place, and this time I wasn't posing as a private investigator.

Slipping around the corner to the kitchen, I headed toward the kangaroo by the microwave. Something was strange about its eyes too. Though the rest of the figurine was painted, its eyes were glossy black balls, like something a taxidermist would use.

I turned it over in my hands. A brown circular felt sticker covered the bottom. It looked similar to the adhesive felt pads I often placed on the bottom of furniture to prevent scratches to hardwood floors.

I frowned. Was there a hole in the bottom of this kangaroo too?

My ringtone sounded, piercing the silence in the kitchen. Chip howled, seeming quite displeased with the rude awakening.

"Chip!" I sang in the most soothing voice I could manage. "Shush, baby. It's only my phone. It's—" I looked at my caller ID—

"It's Officer Appley. Everything's fine." I patted my leg and Chip came running, his howls now soft whimpers. "Hello?"

"Miss Hadley, it's Dennis Appley. I tried calling this morning. Got some news for you." He sounded upbeat.

I slid my nail under the edge of the felt sticker on the bottom of the kangaroo. "Oh? Did you arrest someone?" The sticker peeled off easily, exposing a round plastic plug protruding slightly from a hole. Just like the hole in the kangaroo upstairs.

"No arrest yet, but we believe we found the car that side-swiped you. It's a dark blue BMW and the last letter of the license plate is a D, which fits with your supremely vague description of the vehicle."

I pinched the plastic plug with my nails and pulled. The plug popped out, along with two thin, black wires. *What?* Wires inside the kangaroo? "That's weird," I muttered, looking inside the hole.

"Indeed it is. Especially since it was Marian's car."

"Wait." I redirected my attention to Officer Appley. "You said the person who sideswiped me was in *Marian's* car?"

"Yes, ma'am. Her car had two separate impact areas on the right side. It looks almost as bad as your aunt's car. A neighbor saw it parked in front of Marian's house early this morning."

"Any idea who was driving the car?" I asked, frowning at the small wires hanging out of the kangaroo. I tugged on them and a small black circuit-looking device came out.

"This is an open investigation so I can't say too much, but we do have a couple of leads," he continued. "Everyone is at the station today working on the homicide case, as well as last night's incident involving you."

My stomach flip-flopped. "So you think the two crimes are connected?"

"I can't share that information."

"Right. Of course not." I studied the electronic innards I'd just removed. Why was there a circuit inside the kangaroo?

I recalled my conversation with Phillip Friday night. He had said Kent owned a small electronics company. I had interpreted that to mean his company was small, but I realized now he'd actually said Kent owned a small-electronics company. As in, a company that makes small electronics.

I guessed the kangaroo in my hands was an electronic toy or gadget that Kent had created, but I couldn't tell what purpose it served. It must have been what he was trying to make in the room upstairs when he broke one and threw it in the trash. And considering the entire armoire of kangaroos, he was probably planning to drill holes in a bunch of them and stuff them with electronics, if he hadn't already.

But what was it? A kitchen device? A timer, or perhaps an accessory for his fancy three-in-one cooker? I studied the many-faceted circuit board. On the top, a tiny light blinked every several seconds, casting a green glow on a metal piece the size of a grain of rice that looked like a microphone.

I dropped the kangaroo, shattering its head. "Oh my goodness!" I said, a jolt of fear shocking my nerves. It wasn't a kitchen gadget. It was some sort of listening device.

"Oh my goodness is right," Appley said. "We're trying to locate Marian's roommate to question her about this. What can you tell me about Ms. Celine McCarron?"

"Celine is…" I trailed off, staring at the shattered figurine on the counter. The two eyes, connected by red wires leading to the small black box, weren't eyes at all. They were miniature cameras.

The kangaroo had been watching me. *Kent,* I presumed, had been watching me.

Did this mean he had used this kangaroo cam—or one of the dozen others upstairs—to spy on Marian? Had he seen footage of her with Phillip?

My stomach lurched. If Kent knew Marian was cheating on him, would it have angered him enough to kill her?

I shook my head. Kent was in Philly the whole time. His

customer, Beau, had confirmed it when he said he walked Kent to his room when he got drunk at the gala, which was the same night Marian went missing.

I replayed the conversation with Beau in my mind. Beau hadn't seemed to mind helping Kent walk up to his room; in fact, he seemed to enjoy the excuse to get away from the boring gala for a while. Beau said he even considered pretending to be drunk so he, too, could escape the gala.

I straightened my back. What if *Kent* had faked being drunk and then driven back to Darlington Hills to kill Marian? If he had been tracking her then he would have known exactly where she was.

"Officer Appley, how far of a drive is it from Philly to Darlington Hills?"

"Five to six hours, depending on traffic. Why?"

Kent had returned my calls at 8:30 a.m. the next day. It was possible he left Philly in the early evening, driven to Darlington Hills and killed Marian, and then driven back to Philly in the span of ten or so hours.

"And when the police officer found Marian in the creek, did she have her car keys with her?"

"I can't share that information," he said. "Why do you want to know? I can talk to our detective and see if he feels comfortable sharing—"

"I don't care if this is police business!" I shrieked. "I need to know right this second. Did she have her keys with her and was there a dog keychain attached?"

Every moment that passed was torture. Instinct told me to run but fear turned my legs into two-ton steel poles, incapable of movement.

"What's going on? Where are you?" he asked. His voice was filled with concern.

"I'm at Kent's. Tell me, did she or didn't she have her keys?"

He cleared his throat. "Do not repeat this, but the victim was found with her purse, which did contain her car keys. They're currently locked away in our evidence room at the station, which means someone has a spare set of keys. Have you had any subsequent conversations with Marian's roommate since I questioned you on Friday?"

"Was there a dog keychain with her keys?" I demanded.

"Hang on. I'm looking through the photos. Computer's running slow today."

I looked out the windows along the back of the house, spotting my handbag on one of the swivel chairs.

Go outside, I told myself. *Get your bag and leave*. It was thirty, maybe forty steps away, but the distance to my bag seemed so much farther, like a treacherous journey I wasn't sure I wanted to take. But I had to leave. If I was wrong about Kent, I could apologize later.

I turned both feet toward the back door, then put my right foot in front of the other. *Must leave the house*. If Kent had the tools and know-how to turn the kangaroo into a surveillance camera, he could have put a tracking device in the keychain he'd given Marian. Maybe he'd been tracking her for a long time because he was a creep, and that's how he learned she was cheating on him. Or maybe he started spying on her because he had become suspicious.

What else had Kent bugged? The peculiar-looking ceramic cat that he gave Erin when they dated? He'd given it to her while they were dating.

My heart hammered against my rib cage as though it were trying to escape. I slipped my hand into my back pocket and removed the mystery pen I'd found in my handbag. I twisted it in the middle to unscrew it.

On the other end of the phone, Officer Appley muttered to himself while clicking repeatedly on what I guessed was his mouse.

I gave one final twist and the two halves of the pen separated.

Wrapped around a thin plastic tube of ink was a red wire, just like the one in the kangaroo. The wire was connected to a tiny black circuit-looking device about the size of a raisin, which had a tiny battery affixed to it.

I raised my arm to throw the pen, but stopped myself. The police might need it as evidence. "Officer Appley?" I said, screwing the pen back together and jamming in my pocket. "You there?"

"No doggie keychain," he announced. "But there is a small kangaroo keychain. I can see how someone might mistake it for a dog. Looks like a cheap little trinket."

I yanked opened the kitchen drawer under the microwave as another thought occurred to me. My hands shaking, I rummaged through the random assortment of items inside.

Under a slew of pens and a spiral notebook was a set of keys.

"You said Marian had a BMW?" I confirmed.

"That's right. Why?"

"I just found a set of car keys in one of Kent's drawers. There's a BMW logo on the key remote."

"They aren't Kent's car keys?"

"No. He drives a Ford truck." I threw the keys in the drawer, slammed it shut, and ran toward the back door. "And I think I know what all the kangaroos were for. He put a bug of some sort, like a tracking device, in them. He also bugged a pen and dropped it in my purse yesterday. I'd bet he also bugged the kangaroo on Marian's key chain."

Officer Appley swore. "A GPS tracker. Get out of Kent's house. *Now*."

CHAPTER EIGHTEEN

Kent had bugged me. He had bugged Marian. He killed Marian. He tried to kill me.

My body exploding with panic, I raced toward the chair by the pool and seized my handbag. Something hard rammed into the middle of my back, making me yell out in pain. My feet left the ground, my bag flew from my hand, and I saw the pool below me half a second before I plunged into it.

As soon as my feet hit the bottom, I shoved off the tiled surface, rocketing toward the top. But two hands stopped me midway, forcing me back down. Someone was in the pool with me. Trying to drown me.

I wasn't far from the surface—the pool wasn't that deep—but the blurry form standing in front of me was squeezing the life out of my shoulders, making sure I didn't return to the top for more oxygen.

I kicked and punched, twisted and writhed to get out from under the hands on my shoulders. My lungs burned. I'd only had time to suck in half a breath, if that much, before I hit the water.

Silver stars dotted my vision, growing in number by the second. Fighting the figure in front of me was no use; my attacker was far stronger than me. My punches were futile, my nails were clipped short, and no one would hear me if I screamed underwater. All my God-given natural defense mechanisms were useless.

The pen, I recalled, momentarily pausing my thrashing. *I still have the pen Kent bugged.*

I reached around and yanked it from my back pocket, clutching it tightly so it wouldn't slip out of my shaking hands.

Without hesitating, I aimed the pointy end toward my attacker, squeezed my eyes shut, and stabbed it into the person as hard as I could. Exactly where I stabbed, I didn't want to know, but the blurry form simultaneously yelled and released my shoulders.

I sprang off the bottom of the pool once again, this time angling away from my attacker. Above the water's surface, I sucked in the deepest, fastest breath of air possible. Three fierce swim strokes later, I was at the back corner of the pool, scrambling out of the water with lightning speed.

"You're *dead*, Hadley!" It was Kent's voice.

I didn't dare waste time looking back at him. A series of grunts and splashes told me he was getting out of the pool and it wouldn't take him long to reach me. That, and I didn't want to see my pen half-dangling from any part of him.

Running for the driveway was not an option because Kent was between me and the gate. I scanned the backyard, evaluating my options. The fence was too high to climb and there wasn't another gate.

Instead, I aimed for the pool equipment shed. As I ran, I screamed so loudly it felt like my throat was ripping. Kent's yard backed up to a small forest, but there was a chance a neighbor on either side of him would hear me.

Approaching the shed, I kept my eyes on the roll-up door. Kent hadn't put the new lock I bought on the latch yet, so I could, in theory, open it. Question was, could I keep Kent out once I was inside?

The sound of his footsteps tearing through the grass behind me told me I hadn't injured him too badly with the pen. I'd probably just made him angrier.

Unable to control my momentum, I slid across the mossy stone pavers in front of the shed and slammed into the thin metal door, causing the entire structure to rattle. I gripped the handle and in one swift motion, rolled up the door high enough to scurry inside.

The door rumbled as I shoved it back down to the ground. Darkness surrounded me and panic consumed me. Any moment now, Kent would reach the door. There was no way I could prevent him from opening it. I couldn't lock it from the inside and even if I tried to counter his force when he pulled the door up and open, I wouldn't be able to out-muscle him.

I whipped my head in the direction of the pile of floats. Without any windows in the shed, it was too dark to see. I lunged blindly to my right with outstretched arms. My fingers brushed against something rough and round. The pool noodle.

I yanked it from the pile and dashed back toward the door.

It was a roll-up door just like those in Aunt Deb's storage facility: a thin metal curtain that coiled around an overhead horizontal bar when raised. She had complained on more than one occasion about tenants who filled their units with so much stuff that something got lodged in the coiling mechanism, which prevented the door from rolling up.

Raising the pool noodle above my head, I felt for the narrow gap between the roller bar and metal door and thrust the noodle up into it as hard as I could. It was jammed tightly in there, but I didn't know how long it would keep him out. The pool noodle was made of foam; Kent was made of muscles.

Using all my remaining strength, I pushed against the door, ready to resist its upward force in case the pool noodle failed. My right foot found something sturdy directly across from where I stood—the pool filter, I guessed—and I wedged myself between it and the door, bracing for impact.

The hit came a second later, sending painful shock waves through my back and neck. The shed shook so much I thought it would collapse. I felt like the little pig hiding from the Big Bad Wolf in the home built of straw. Only there was nowhere else I could run if he huffed and puffed his way inside.

There was a brief moment of silence, followed by more rattling. The door began to rise and light pierced into the dark shed. He was raising the door.

The coiling mechanism above me screeched in protest at the foamy obstruction. Kent, grunting loudly, shook the door vigorously. I held onto the pool noodle, making sure it didn't wiggle free.

Kent lowered the door back to the ground and jerked it up again, but it didn't raise more than an inch.

"What'd you do to my door, woman?" he bellowed. The door dropped to the ground, leaving me in darkness once again.

I ignored Kent and continued pushing against the door. He would ram it again and I had to be ready. The pool noodle seemed to be preventing him from raising it, but I didn't know if the thin metal would withstand another one of his powerful blows. It seemed flimsier than the storage shed doors at Aunt Deb's facility.

"You think you have the right to pry into my personal life?" he said. "I knew I couldn't trust you. First you withheld information from me about someone intruding into *my* house, and then you lied to me about visiting your childhood friend Anna at the hotel. Guess you didn't know that her husband is the local pharmacist. The two of them moved here several months ago." His voice sounded more distant, as though he were walking away from the shed. Most likely, he was getting a running start for his next attempt to plow into the door. "You were snooping into my business, Hadley. You're gonna wish you hadn't."

Kent rammed into the door again. A fresh wave of pain tore through my neck and back, making me yelp. The shed lit up again, this time from a sliver of light along the side of the door. I turned my head and inspected the damage. Not good. The thin metal was dented, part of the door knocked off its tracks.

I continued to press my back against the door and my foot against the filtering unit as I scanned the shed's contents: pool equipment, a half-used bag of mulch, floats, and a bucket of left-over paint from the shed's recent paint job. Unfortunately, there were no shovels, baseball bats, or anything else I could use for self-defense.

I needed to stall Kent long enough for the police to arrive—at least I hoped they were on their way. Officer Appley had told me to get out of Kent's house, so I prayed he hadn't assumed I left and decided to look for me elsewhere.

"Let me get this straight," I said. "You put a tracking device in my purse, then ran me off the road last night and tried to kill me because I lied to you about Anna?" I hoped I could buy myself more time with conversation. "Isn't that rather harsh for one tiny fib?"

He barked out a laugh. "One *tiny* fib," he repeated, mocking me. "When my friends lie to me, I no longer trust them. And you and I both know that you know too much about my personal situation."

"By 'personal situation,' you're referring to the fact that you killed your fiancée?"

"I loved Marian! I wanted to give her the world, but she didn't appreciate anything I did for her. Not the trips to Australia, the giant engagement ring I bought her—nothing! She wouldn't have cheated on me if she had been grateful."

He was hollering. Good. Hopefully his neighbors would hear

him and come over to see what was going on. I needed to make him angrier so he would continue to yell.

"You didn't love Marian. You were obsessed. So much so that you stalked her with all your weird little kangaroos." Tensing my muscles, I braced for him to ram the door again. I couldn't let down my guard.

"You nosey little snoot! Marian cheated on her ex-husband when she and I met, so I had to make sure she wouldn't do the same to me. She traveled a lot for business—or so she claimed—and during her last trip, she told me she had a customer dinner in New York. Imagine how I felt when I checked Mary Lou's location and found her back in Darlington Hills."

"Mary Lou was the kangaroo on Marian's keychain?" I asked.

He pounded a fist against the door. "Yes, and Mary Lou was supposed to be at an Italian restaurant in New York City, not in Darlington Hills!" His voice rose even higher than before.

Why hadn't his neighbors come by to see what was causing all the commotion?

"When I found out she'd flown home without telling me, I *knew* she was cheating on me. But I never would have guessed it was with her ex-husband. She deserved those bullets I gave her!"

My heart ached for poor Marian. I recalled the afternoon she walked into Kent's backyard with the kangaroo keychain—aka Mary Lou, the GPS tracking device—dangling from her fingers. If only she hadn't brought it on her business trip.

Kent plowed into the roll-up door, widening the gap along the side. More light poured inside.

I considered the shed's contents. The bag of mulch wasn't full enough to do me any good, and the pool floats certainly wouldn't inflict any pain. My gaze fell upon the can of paint. If it were heavy enough, maybe I could hit him with it if he pushed open the door. It would be better than nothing.

"I have two more bullets," Kent said, his mouth near the gap between the door and wall. "This time, they have *your* name on them."

"Sure, why don't you go get your gun? I'll wait right here while you go inside to get it," I said sarcastically. I was certain if he'd had his gun with him he would have used it by now. "If you hurt me, the police will know it was you."

"No they won't. My truck is at the deli and I'm waiting on the order I just placed. It's a little thing called an alibi."

"Yeah, except you can't pull the same trick twice in one week and expect to get away with it. Last time, you feigned being drunk and then drove home and killed Marian. What'd you do, rent a car for that trip?"

"I borrowed keys to a rental car from some woman at the gala. Took them right outta her purse in her chair while she was dancing. She was even more drunk than I was pretending to be. Then I drove back here, tracked Marian, and waited ever so patiently for her outside Hotel Darlington. Her ex-husband walked her out as far as the hotel's parking lot before he went back inside. What kind of man lets a woman walk home by herself in the middle of the night?"

Kent grunted as he tried raising the door again. It creaked and rattled, but didn't budge.

Engaging every muscle in my body, I pressed my back against the door and my foot against the pool filter. A cracking sound came from the unit, but it continued to support my weight.

"Please don't break," I whispered. If the filter moved and I lost my leverage, he might have an easier time forcing open the door.

Kent swore, then stopped pulling up on the door handle. I looked in the direction of the paint can. Now was the perfect time to retrieve it. I had to take the chance. He would strike again any second now, and the metal door could buckle at any moment. I needed something to defend myself.

I lunged toward the paint can and grabbed it with two hands, ready to throw it if Kent busted inside.

But he remained quiet.

I returned to my guard position, pressing my back against the door and my foot on the filter.

Where was he? Had he been serious about getting his gun?

Terror surged through me, making it difficult to suck in a full breath. I gripped the paint can tighter. It was heavy, but it wouldn't do diddly squat if bullets started flying. Running my fingers along the crusty dried paint surrounding the can's lid, I considered another strategy.

I needed to pop off the lid.

There was an explosive bang against the door, stopping my heart.

A bullet?

No. A bullet would have gone through the door. This was something else. It wasn't a fist or foot; it sounded different than his previous hits.

The banging came again, this time a series of consecutive strikes.

Grunting, Kent thrust himself against the door, widening the opening on the side. I pressed my foot against the filter, pushing as hard I could to counter his force. My back ached and my legs shook from fear and fatigue.

A metallic clattering sounded to my left and a long, thin pole slid through the opening in the door. It was the cast iron curtain rod the crew had hung this morning. He was using it as a lever to widen the gap.

I dug my nails around the edges of the paint can's lid, trying to pry it open. The dried, crusty paint was like super glue holding the lid in place.

Another cracking sound came from the filter, and the piece of equipment slid away from me. With both my feet now on floor of the shed, I didn't have nearly as much leverage against Kent.

The tips of my fingers burned as I pried at the can. One side gave and I pulled as hard as I could, certain I was ripping off my nails in the process.

Kent worked the pole up and down the side of the door, peeling it away from its roller tracks. The gap was now large enough to climb through.

Roaring with anger, he gave a sudden forceful thrust against the door. It buckled in the middle. He stuck a foot through the gap, followed by the rest of his leg and then a hand.

Summoning all my focus and energy into the four fingers on my right hand, I pried the lid from the paint. I dashed to the side of the door, holding the can in front of me.

Without my resistance against the door, the gap increased and Kent flew inside the shed, tripping over the curtain rod that clattered to the concrete floor. But he regained his balance immediately and whipped around to face me.

I heaved the open end of the can toward him, dousing his face with yellow paint. "Kangaroo psycho!" I screamed.

His eyes coated with paint, he lunged for me blindly.

He missed.

I ran.

I didn't slow down until I was halfway down his street, where I was greeted by ferociously swirling red and blue lights atop two approaching patrol cars, their sirens blaring.

I'd never heard a more beautiful sound.

CHAPTER NINETEEN

It was splurge time. After nearly drowning yesterday and coming frighteningly close to the pearly white gates, I treated myself to the most decadent, sugary treat available at Whisks and Whiskers: the Paw-some Brownie Raspberry Cheesecake.

I slid the side of my fork through the swirled buttercream icing, down through the fluffy cheesecake and then into the thick double-chocolate brownie. I brought the bite towards my mouth, which was watering with anticipation.

I closed my eyes as I chewed. "This is incredible, Erin. I couldn't have asked for a better last meal here. My belly will be happy and full when I fly home this afternoon." The rest of my body, however, would likely not enjoy the flight. My legs and back felt like I'd done a thousand squats with two-hundred-pound weights. But thankfully, I didn't have any serious injuries from yesterday.

"Glad you like it!" Erin said. "Although I'm surprised you didn't catch the first flight out of here this morning after what happened yesterday."

"Don't give her any ideas," Aunt Deb pleaded. Then, turning to me, she removed her fork from her own slice of cheesecake and shook it at me. "Hadley, hon, I don't like your choice of words. This is not your last meal in Darlington Hills. Even if you don't get the job, you will have plenty of opportunities to come visit." Her words were blubbery with impending tears. "I'm sure they don't make cheesecake this good in New Orleans, so you'll have to come back soon, you hear? Just say the word, and I'm certain Erin will make some for you." She glanced at Erin from the side of her eye. "And if not, I will."

I reached across the table and grabbed Aunt Deb's hand, giving it a squeeze. "There are more far important things than cheesecake in Darlington Hills. Don't worry, I'll visit you soon."

In fact, there was a good chance I would have to return soon to testify against Kent, who would be waking up this morning in a local jail cell. I'd given my official statement to the police yesterday, but I was awaiting confirmation on whether my presence would be required at his trial.

For now, I needed to return to New Orleans. I had to keep working for my current employer to pay the bills until I found another job. I was certain Kent never intended for me to deposit the fat check he gave me—how could I if I were dead?—but I deposited it last night anyway using the banking app on my phone.

I didn't want to wait and risk not getting paid. Although I had planned to spend the extra money I'd made from Kent's project on moving expenses and a new handbag, I gave nearly all of it to Aunt Deb for her car. The body shop said they could repair it, but Aunt Deb had a hefty insurance deductible to pay.

I spent the remainder of Kent's check this morning on some toys and food for Chip, who Aunt Deb had insisted on fostering when the folks from the animal shelter removed him from his home. She would probably end up adopting Chip, since Kent would likely go to prison after his trial.

"Well, ladies, today is a new day, and we have a lot to be thankful for," Aunt Deb said. "Firstly, that you're alive and well,

Hadley." She turned her blue eyes on me, her smile brightening our side of the café. "Secondly, the disturbing cat figurine that usually sits by the cash register is gone. Life is good, I tell you."

Erin leaned forward, resting her elbows on the table. "After you called me last night about what happened with Kent and the tracking devices, I drove over here and threw the cat he gave me on the floor. Sure enough, there were wires and a small circuit board inside."

Aunt Deb gave a low whistle. "I knew that cat was possessed."

A pained expression crossed Erin's face. "Just think what could have happened if I hadn't met Rhett. What if I'd dated Kent longer?"

"But you didn't," I said. "You ended up with Rhett and there's no need to worry about all the what-ifs."

She nodded, seeming to consider my advice. "I told Rhett everything. I put Peter in charge of the café yesterday morning and took Rhett out for a breakfast picnic at a park along the James River, and told him I was dating Kent when he and I met. I confessed everything to him."

"And? What'd he say?" Aunt Deb asked, now engrossed in Erin's story. A fire alarm could have sounded and she wouldn't have bothered evacuating until Erin finished talking.

Erin smiled sheepishly. "Rhett said the important thing was that I chose him," she said. "He pointed out that I made it clear who I wanted to be with when I decided to finish my dinner with Rhett after Kent passed by our table in the restaurant."

Aunt Deb nodded decisively. "Sounds like you've found yourself a good man."

"The absolute best," Erin agreed.

My eyes widened. "I wonder if Kent was tracking you that evening he caught you with Rhett."

Erin shuddered. "I don't want to think about that possibility. I'm freaked out enough as it is after learning the cat he gave me was bugged."

Erin stopped talking at the sound of a nearby hiss. A slender white cat with dark gray ears and a striped tail swatted at King Oliver, who was trying to nudge the cat off its spot on the top tier of a carpeted play structure.

Erin stood and rushed over to break up the dispute. "King Oliver! Mind your manners! You know better than this." She reached down and carefully lifted the white cat. "It's okay, girl. King Oliver can be a bit of a grouch sometimes."

She returned to the table, cuddling the cat under her chin. The cat turned its head toward me.

"Her eyes are so blue," I said, unable to stop looking at her precious little face.

"Here, why don't you hold her?" Erin placed the cat in my arms before I could object. "This one's a sweetheart. She's a Siamese-tabby mix, about two years old. She'll probably jump down in a few seconds. Most cats do."

But the cat stayed put, nuzzling her face into my arm. "You *are* a sweet girl, aren't you?" I cooed. My brownie raspberry cheesecake remained half-eaten in front of me, but I didn't dare take a bite. I didn't want to move and make the cat jump down. Holding her and listening to the low rumble of her purring was the only thing I wanted to do at the moment. The cake could wait.

"So let me get this straight," Aunt Deb said, turning to Erin. "Your boyfriend works for Kent?"

Erin nodded. "For now he does. We'll see what happens if —*when*—Kent goes to prison."

My phone rang. Trying not to disturb the cat, I slowly shifted her to my left arm and reached into my bag with the other hand, fishing for my phone.

Four rings later, I pulled it out and checked the caller ID. "It's Vincent!"

"Good morning, this is Hadley," I answered, my pulse soaring with anticipation.

"Hadley, this is Vincent Weatherford from Walnut Ridge. Do you have a minute?"

"Absolutely." I tried to keep my tone casual, as though I hadn't been desperately awaiting his call.

"Good. I wanted to let you know that I have made a decision on the interior designer for the new Walnut Ridge catalog. After much deliberation, I am pleased to offer you the job. Congratulations, and I hope you will accept this position."

"Yes, I would love to!" I exclaimed, giving Aunt Deb and Erin a spirited thumbs-up. "Thank you so much. I can't wait to get started." If I hadn't been holding the cat, I would have jumped up and down in the booth.

"Good, because I'll need you to start in the next couple of weeks. We have a lot of work to do before the publication of my first printed catalog. Will the timing be an issue?"

"Not at all. I'll start packing the minute I get home." I was a pro at moving. I could have all my stuff in boxes in less than three days, ready for the moving company to load onto their truck.

"If you have time before your flight today, I'll need you to come by and sign some paperwork," he said, his tone slightly more upbeat than it was during my interview. "I also have some Walnut Ridge-branded swag for you. Nothing big, just some pens and a tote bag."

I lifted my eyebrows. Tote bag? This day kept getting better and better. "Thank you, I can be there at noon."

"Good. The salary will be as advertised in the job posting, with insurance benefits and two weeks of vacation. Any questions?"

"None right now. I can't wait to join your team. I thought I'd blown it when I didn't answer your math question."

"You gave the correct answer," he said dryly.

"I did?"

He sighed. "The response I wanted to hear was 'I don't know.' When you work for me, if I ask you a question and you don't

LEMON YELLOW LIES

know the answer, I don't want you giving me some baloney response. Nothing irritates me more. Instead, you will need to say you don't know but will find out. It's as simple as that."

Whew! This guy would be fun to work for. "Yes, I understand. You won't hear any baloney coming from me."

I thanked him once more, hung up, and squealed. "I am officially moving to Darlington Hills!" I celebrated again after hearing myself say it out loud. The town I adored so much would become my home in one week.

Jumping from her seat, Aunt Deb leaned across the table with her arms open, then stopped midway and laughed. "Looks like you and your new friend have something in common." She motioned to the cat.

I looked down to find the cat enthusiastically licking my cheesecake.

"She likes that cake as much as you do," Erin said, wiggling her eyebrows up and down. "You know, the rep from the animal shelter is sitting at the table in the corner if you want to adopt her."

I leaned close to the cat and tickled under her chin. "How would you like to live with me?" I asked. "You sure do love brownie raspberry cheesecake, don't you, girl?"

"I'm telling you, it's a sign," Erin said. "The adoption table is ten steps away."

"You know what? I would like to have a cat," I said. "And this sweet girl has melted my heart into a puddle of love. She'll have to wait a week or so until I move here, but I'm signing the paperwork today before anyone else adopts her. Just as soon as she finishes licking my dessert."

Erin clapped her hands excitedly. "I promise I'll take good care of her before you move here, although I can't say I'll let her eat off any more customer's plates. She's violating like a gazillion health codes right now."

I gently pulled the cat away from my cake, giving her a hug.

"You hear that, sweetie? You get to come home with me soon." I brushed off a piece of fruit from one of her whiskers. "I'm going to name you Razzy, short for raspberry."

The hum of Razzy's purring intensified, telling me she liked her name. She was happy and I was happy. It was yet another thing we had in common.

Despite the traumatic events of the past week, my heart tingled with excitement of what was soon to come: a new cat, new friends, new job, and a new life in Darlington Hills.

THE END

Thanks so much for reading my book! I truly hope you enjoyed it. If so, can you please spend a couple of minutes leaving a review? It would mean the world to me, and it helps other cozy mystery fans learn more about this book.

Love Hadley Home Design Cozy Mysteries? Keep turning the pages for an excerpt from the next book in the series, *Pearl White Peril*.

NEWSLETTER SIGNUP

Join my community of readers! You'll receive exclusive subscriber deals and giveaways, recipes and other fun printables, behind-the-scenes peeks, and news about upcoming releases. You can unsubscribe at any time.

Go to subscribepage.com/emilynewsletter or scan the QR code below with your phone's camera.

BOOK #2 PREVIEW — PEARL WHITE PERIL

Chapter One

Two champagne-gold pendant lights, suspended directly above the kitchen island, cast a warm glow on the glossy marble countertops and subway tile backsplash. The all-white kitchen in the Walnut Ridge home gleamed with cheerful opulence, despite the untimely arrival of a mid-morning storm. Persistent waves of rain thrashed against the window above the sink, almost drowning out the angry chants of protestors in the backyard.

I approached the counter space between the stove and refrigerator and adjusted the items on a woven rattan tray, moving the stack of salad plates in front of the wooden cake stand and vase of lavender hydrangeas. The plates were part of the company's new Stantonville dinnerware set, and it was best to put them in the spotlight.

I turned around and surveyed the room. "Hey, Terence," I called out over my shoulder. "Can you please move the middle barstool a smidgeon to the right? I need it centered between the other two."

Terence Holt wiped his palms against his jeans as he walked

from the adjoining breakfast room toward the island. "You got it." He slid the low-back stool toward its neighbor then raised an eyebrow at me. "Good?"

"Yes, thank you. You know I couldn't do this without you. Everything looks perfect." Terence and his crew were the company muscles, doing everything from moving furniture and painting walls to hanging drapes, shelves, lights and artwork. They transformed rooms within the Walnut Ridge home two, sometimes three times a day, making them look completely different. And fortunately, Terence was a pro at interpreting words like 'smidgeon.'

He tapped his knuckles against the white marble. "You'd better hope the rain lets up. What's on the other side of that window is just plain ugly. We might as well be taking photos at night, it's so dark out there." As he spoke, one of his braids fell in his face. The sides of his head were shaved, but the top held a thick stack of long black braids, which he usually tied back with a band.

I grinned and joined Terence by the stools. "Nah, don't worry about the storm. The graphics team can spiff up that window faster than you can say Photoshop. They'll make it look like the clear-sky Spring day we should be having right now." The day's forecast promised a full day of rain, and we couldn't afford to delay the photo shoot.

It was early April, and Walnut Ridge's first-ever printed catalog was scheduled to arrive in mailboxes throughout the country on July 1. The tight deadline meant long workdays, including some Saturdays. We had started staging rooms and shooting pictures several weeks ago and we had at least five more weeks to go for the first issue.

But I didn't complain about the long hours. I loved nearly every aspect of my new, never-dreamed-it-could-happen-to me job.

"There you are," said a voice behind me. Terence and I turned as Vincent Weatherford, owner of Walnut Ridge Furniture and Decor, pushed his way past a tower of plastic storage bins and stepped into the kitchen. In a pressed blue dress shirt buttoned nearly to the top and well-worn dark blue jeans, his style wavered somewhere between smart and casual without directly hitting the trendy smart-casual look.

When Vincent started Walnut Ridge six years ago, customers could only order from his company's website. But when every southern woman became obsessed with his furniture and decor, Vincent decided to escape the digital confines of his website and mail monthly catalogs to customers.

He moved from Baltimore to Darlington Hills, Virginia nine months ago and bought a seventy-year old classic southern home with a wrap-around porch, columns, and black shutters that contrasted nicely with the smooth white siding. His was one of the larger homes in the ritzy, heavily wooded North Hills neighborhood.

Vincent's gaze settled on Terence. "Don't you keep your phone on? I've been looking for you the past five minutes. I should have known Hadley had ensnared you in conversation. I need you to go do something about *them*."

Vincent jerked his head toward the kitchen window. Half a dozen drenched protestors held soggy posters condemning the new catalog for killing trees. It was the same group that had been protesting outside for the past several weeks. Two men blew into long plastic noisemaker horns, while Sonya Bean, the leader of the six, shouted into a white bullhorn.

Terence, who was a month away from graduating from Old Dominion University with a psychology degree, was certainly the most qualified person on Vincent's payroll to try to reason with the protestors, but I guessed Vincent picked him because he was also the most physically intimidating, with his six-three frame and bodybuilder biceps.

"Go tell them I'm calling the cops if they don't get off my

lawn," Vincent said. "They're going to tear up the grass with all this rain."

Terence nodded and started walking toward the kitchen door, which led to the backyard.

"Remind them they're on private property," Vincent called after him. "Make sure they move to the street out front, or better yet, help them find their way out of this neighborhood."

"Help them find their inner child," I teased. "Go make Freud proud."

Laughing, Terence stepped out into the downpour.

Vincent's eyes swept across the kitchen. "How much more time do you need to finish staging the kitchen? Rachael is wrapping up photos in the entry hall, and her crew is shooting this room next. You did see today's itinerary, right? It said kitchen photos at ten-thirty. It's ten-fifteen now, and you clearly have a lot more work to do."

I straightened my back. "Actually, I'm done with the kitchen. I just finished arranging the Stantonville plates—"

"Done?" Vincent's eyes were wide. "I'm putting the kitchen on the cover of my new catalog. For some people, this room will be their first impression of Walnut Ridge. I cannot have them thinking I sell soulless junk. This kitchen should scream contemporary southern, but right now it's more of a sad whimper. Give me some warm dashes of color, Hadley. I need a kitchen that begs for lively Sunday brunches with maple pancakes and griddled country ham. This room should be so southern that it conjures Scarlett O'Hara herself and makes her cry tears of sweetened peach iced tea. Can you do that for me?"

I forced myself to hold his gaze while I took a slow, steady breath. "Of course." I strode toward the storage bin marked "serving dishes" and removed a small glass bowl. Tucking it under my left arm like a football, I moved across the kitchen to Vincent's refrigerator, scanned the well-stocked shelves, and removed five lemons from the fruit drawer. I set the bowl on the counter by the sink, stacked the lemons in a pyramid, then swung around toward Vincent, my wavy ponytail whipping across my face.

"There," I said.

He brought his hand to his face and massaged the gray and black bristles of his goatee. In the weeks since I had moved to Darlington Hills to work as Walnut Ridge's lead interior designer, I had learned Vincent was never pleased with anyone's work initially, no matter how good it was. He first ridiculed it and then educated us on how we should have done it. But I tried to not let his criticism bring me down; he was probably just nervous about his first catalog.

The deep creases between Vincent's eyes softened. "This is more like it. It's sophisticated yet sensible. Go tell Rachael we're ready to shoot the kitchen."

The back door opened and a soaked Terence walked through, followed by an older man, perhaps in his sixties, wearing a red raincoat that looked about three sizes too large for his slender frame. Next to me, Vincent swore.

The man's eyes fell on Vincent. "You are in a heap of trouble, Mr. Weatherford. Don't think just because you aren't responding to my violation notices that I'm going to back down."

"You can't just walk into my house whenever you'd like," Vincent said. "We're in the middle of a photo shoot. If you have an issue with my business, get in line. Go make yourself a sign and join the tree-loving group outside."

The man flipped his jack hood back, revealing frizzy silver hair. He marched toward Vincent and me. "I don't care about trees. I care about rules. And as a new resident of North Hills neighborhood, you are required to abide by the rules set forth by the homeowner's association. Pursuant to Article Twelve, Section Four in the HOA's governing covenants, residents are not allowed to run a business from their home without prior approval."

My mouth fell open. Vincent hadn't gotten approval to run his business from his home?

The man glanced at me and gave a curt nod. "Willy Ellsworth, president of North Hills HOA. I assume you work with Mr. Weatherford?"

Before I could respond or offer my hand to introduce myself, Willy returned his fiery eyes to Vincent. "Given the nature of your business and the fact that you did not seek prior approval, I can assure you my board will not allow you to conduct your business in our upstanding neighborhood. We will take action against you, Mr. Weatherford."

Not good. If the HOA forced Vincent to cease business operations, we wouldn't finish photos for the catalog in time. Or worse, Vincent would be forced to move and I might not have a steady job anymore. Although my plan for moving to Virginia involved starting my own interior design consulting business, my only clients so far were my Aunt Deb and good friend Carmella, neither of whom I charged for advice. I needed the steady income from Walnut Ridge.

Vincent took a step closer to the man. "I am well aware of your HOA rules. You don't think my attorney reviewed them before I bought this house? Unfortunately for your HOA, its covenants do not give your board any real enforcement power. It's all in the fine print, Willy, and my attorney will be happy to spell it out for you. My company is one of the south's top home furnishing companies, and my neighbors are thrilled to live next to Walnut Ridge's new design home. Besides, it's not like I'm throwing wild parties every night."

"You've had a twenty-foot moving truck parked in front of your house for the past month," Willy said, his voice rising. "Not to mention all the parked cars in front of your home these days, and those hideous storage shed in your side yard which are visible from the street. Your neighbor, Mrs. Feldman, says her five kids can't ride their bikes in this cul-de-sac or play in their front yard because they're scared of that rowdy gang of protestors causing such a hoo-ha in your yard. Your business is a nuisance to this neighborhood."

There was a flicker of light outside, followed immediately by a fierce clap of thunder. The house went dark.

Vincent grumbled, casting an angry look out the window. But as fast as the electricity had cut off, it came back on—except in the kitchen and breakfast room.

Vincent stormed into the breakfast room, looking toward the dining room in the front of the house. Willy and I followed him. "Where did Terence go? He was just in here. Someone needs to go flip the circuit breaker for the kitchen lights. We have a photo shoot in here in less than fifteen minutes."

"He probably went to dry off," I reasoned, turning toward the garage. I could flip the breaker as easily as anyone else. But before I reached the door, one of Terence's guys, Josh Finney, walked into the kitchen carrying a can of paint.

"Go take care of the lights," Vincent barked. I was surprised Vincent hadn't used the opportunity to flip the breaker himself as an excuse to dodge Willy.

Instead, Vincent widened his stance and faced the older man. "You will leave my home immediately or *I* will take action against *you*," he said, punching his words out like a series of rapid, powerful uppercuts. "Do I make myself clear?"

I flinched. Vincent could be moody and condescending, but I'd never seen him act like a rabid Rottweiler before.

Willy removed his raincoat and reached into the front pocket of his shirt, then pulled out an envelope folded in half. "This is a cease and desist letter, curtesy of your neighborhood HOA, which by the way most certainly does have the power to enforce its rules."

Josh popped his head through the doorway and checked the overhead lights. "No good. I flipped the breaker but it didn't do anything. Must be some sort of electrical issue." With his shaggy platinum-blonde hair, tanned skin and paint-streaked sleeveless T-shirt, he resembled a twenty-something-year-old version of Hulk Hogan, only about a quarter of the wrestling star's size. His circa 1980s clear plastic-rimmed eyeglasses had a small smudge of paint on the right lens, and I had to use all my willpower to not march over and clean them myself.

Vincent checked his watch, then dismissed Josh with an impatient flick of his wrist. "Of course it's an electrical issue. You're the handyman; go fix it. Find Terence and get him to help if you can't do it." He stared out the breakfast room's three-panel bay window and shook his head. "This home has been one nightmare after another. It was a junkhouse before I got my hands on it and fixed it up, and despite all the money I dumped into it, this place continues to show its ugly bones."

"I can't believe old Ms. Henkle sold it to you," Willy said. "Considering the price you paid and my dealings with you thus far, I presume you intimidated her into selling."

Vincent yanked the envelope from Willy's hand and tossed it on the breakfast table. "Intimidated? No. I charmed that deed out of her hands." He laughed. "It didn't take much. She probably hadn't been charmed in years."

Terence moseyed back into the breakfast room, his face dry but his solid white T-shirt and blue jeans still soaked. He glanced up at the lights, then looked to Vincent for an explanation.

"Lights out, Josh can't fix it," Vincent said.

"I tried the breaker and nothing happened," Josh explained, his shaky voice obliterating his Hulk Hogan facade. He came and stood next to Terence. "But I can go take care of it."

Terence shook his head. "Thanks, man, but I want you to finish painting the dining room and then move on to the game room. I'll go check it out."

Dropping his eyes to the floor, Josh spun on his heals toward the kitchen.

"Dude. Other way," Terence said, one corner of his mouth lifting into a smile.

Josh shook his head and turned around, revealing already-reddened cheeks. "Right. I get turned around in this place."

"Hadley, tell me the upstairs bedroom is ready for photos," Vincent said. "I don't have time to wait on the lights. We need to keep things rolling. We're finishing everything on today's itinerary even if it means working until midnight."

"It's ready," I responded, thankful I had stayed late last night to stage the room. Whether or not Vincent would think the room was ready was another consideration.

"Terence, go fix the lights," Vincent instructed. "Hadley, follow me upstairs and grab Rachael's crew on the way. Willy, you have ten seconds to leave my house. You will hear from my attorney."

"I'm not going anywhere until you read and acknowledge this cease and desist letter, Mr. Weatherford."

Vincent grabbed the envelope from the table, ripped it in half in one dramatic motion, then threw it back on the table. Grunting, he turned and walked toward the entry hall. I followed, stopping only to ask Rachael to move her team and equipment upstairs.

I caught up to Vincent at the top of the stairs, just as he turned toward the bedroom. "I put some fresh peonies on the nightstand, and I had wanted to add a stack of books with blue spines to complement the cool tones in the Calypso rug, but I couldn't find any in your storage sheds. Do you have any in your bedroom?" Vincent was an avid reader, so there was a good chance he had a few books in his off-limits personal living area, which consumed about half of the home's upstairs space.

The graphics team, which worked remotely from its Detroit office, could easily superimpose a stack of books, but Vincent required all photos to be authentic—wallpaper, paint, and all. He wanted everything to be perfect. Because not only would these photos be printed in the catalog, they would also live in the products section of the company's website. He had never hired an interior designer to stage his furniture for professional photo shoots before, and now he hoped to take Walnut Ridge to the next level.

Vincent stopped walking. "Probably, but I'm not wasting time on that right now. Next time, try the attic. There's a bunch of junk in there from the woman who used to live here. I haven't gone through it but you might find something useful."

Vincent held up a finger, then dug his hand into the back pocket of his jeans and pulled out his vibrating phone. After glancing at the screen, he closed his eyes for a long beat, then brought the phone to his ear. He listened to a deep voice on the other end, clenching the phone so hard his knuckles turned white.

"I don't want any more delays," Vincent snapped. "You need to take care of it this morning." The deep voice continued talking, but Vincent pulled the phone from his ear and hung up.

"Contractor?" I asked.

He resumed walking, his eyes set on the open door in front of us. "No."

I didn't press him to elaborate. It wasn't my business who was on the phone.

Rachael and her crew joined us a minute later, set up their tripods and spotlights, then began shooting the room. After they photographed the bedding collection I had arranged last night, I replaced it with the Augusta Rose duvet cover and matching shams, which featured roses embroidered with stitching several shades darker than the rest of the pink cotton fabric.

The extra-thick synthetic feather insert gave the duvet a nice full shape, and the two additional inserts I hid under the Augusta Rose duvet made the bedding look down right plush. To balance the angular lines of the tufted headboard, I placed a round mirror above the nightstands on both sides of the bed.

Rachael began flitting around the room, snapping photos

from every vantage point possible. She reminded me of Tinker Bell with her asymmetrical pixie cut and spry movements. Leaping from the floor to the chair to the rug to the linen-covered bench at the foot of the bed had never looked so easy. Rachael's two assistants, Silent Kyle and Harry the Hummer, worked alongside her.

Vincent remained quiet as we worked. Not once did he criticize my design choices or tell Rachael how to do her job. He spent more time checking his phone than watching the activity in the room. His eyes followed the photographers without seeming to focus on them. I wondered if Willy had gotten to him, or if the person he had spoken with on the phone had upset him. Or maybe he was just tired. The hypnotic drumming of the rain against the roof and window, interrupted only by the soft clicks of cameras and Harry's soft humming, was enough to put anyone to sleep. It made me want to slide under the stack of warm duvet covers and take a nap.

The harsh screeching of Sonya's bullhorn interrupted my mid-morning nap fantasy. In the front yard, just below the bedroom window, Sonya and her cohorts from the Forest Action League resumed chanting the same words they had chanted for nearly two weeks: "Stop the madness and insanity; kill the catalog, not the trees!"

Their yelling was irritating, but I sympathized with their concerns. I couldn't count the number of catalogs I had thrown away because they weren't relevant. I hoped Walnut Ridge's marketing agency would mail its new catalogs to only the most promising customers.

"If they want to stand in the rain all day and die of pneumonia, that's their business," Vincent said. "But we don't have to listen to them." He propped his phone on a metal stepstool near the door and tapped the big orange play button on his screen, dragging the volume slider all the way to the right. Classical music replaced the chanting instantly, and we enjoyed two entire minutes of a lively piano concerto before a rapid sequence of thwacks interrupted the music.

We all rushed to the window, just as a grapefruit-sized mud ball slammed against the glass.

"They're digging holes out there," Vincent shrieked. "That mud is from my flower beds." He made it to the bedroom door in several large steps. "This madness is going to stop right now. Keep shooting, I am not letting this delay us."

The spirited pounding of Vincent's feet on the stairs was a well-timed accompaniment to the rising crescendo of the classical ballad playing on his phone, punctuated by the swift slamming of the front door.

Rachael and I exchanged eye rolls. Someone yelled below us, but the loud music made it impossible to hear what they were saying. The mud ball assault stopped, and I continued fluffing pillows while Rachael's team snapped away. We finished with the Augusta Rose bedding collection and I went into the room's walk-in closet to retrieve the third and final bedding set that Vincent wanted to include in the catalog. The third set was my favorite and I intended to buy it for my bed once I earned a few paychecks from Walnut Ridge. The soft gray comforter featured evenly spaced pinch pleats, which gave it more depth and texture than any other comforter I'd seen.

"What are you doing?" Rachael asked. She was folding up a tripod. "We need to head downstairs for the next photo shoot." I could barely hear her over the music, but I didn't want to touch Vincent's phone and risk adding to his anger. "We're done in here."

"Vincent wants photos of all three bedding collections," I said, trying to raise my voice loud enough for her to hear me without sounding like I was frustrated. I avoided conflict like I avoided paisley prints and linoleum flooring. Pulling the folded itinerary from the side pocket of my navy tailored skirt, I pointed to the line on the paper that confirmed my belief.

Rachael nodded with a smile. "Yeah, but he told me yesterday he only wants us to shoot the first two bedding sets. Why don't we wait for him to come back up? Should be any minute now."

I frowned. It seemed like Vincent would have told me about the change yesterday before I steamed the comforter and matching pillow shams. "Hold tight, I'll go ask him."

I hurried down the stairs, opened the front door, and stood on the covered front porch while I scanned the yard. Other than an abandoned "kill the catalog" poster by the base of the sprawling oak tree, there were no signs of Vincent, Sonya, or the other protesters. A gust of wind swept a torrent of rain toward the patio, peppering me with cold water. I retreated into the Walnut Ridge home and moved through the family room toward the back door in the kitchen.

A new musical number from Vincent's phone echoed throughout the house, which felt hollow without its typical swarm of frantic workers. I checked my watch. The Walnut Ridge crew stopped work at noon every day, honoring their lunch hour as if it were a religion. But it was only eleven-thirty, too early for lunch.

Curious about where everyone was, I continued exploring downstairs. I stepped into the sunroom, then swung an immediate right through the arched doorway into the dark kitchen. Without the warm glow from the pendant lights, the marble countertops reflected only the muted sunlight from the window above the sink, giving the all-white kitchen a greenish hue.

The back door was open, sprays of rain blowing into the kitchen. Several steps away from the door, the tip of my right shoe kicked something soft. It took me a moment to realize the bright yellow object rolling across the wood floor was a lemon. It settled next to another lemon amid a mess of broken glass and water.

My eyes snapped to the counter space where the glass bowl should have been but wasn't. Questions spun through my mind faster than I could process them. Had someone dropped the bowl of lemons? Why had they been moving it? Why would they leave them on the floor? I couldn't imagine making such a mess and leaving it for someone else to clean up. Who would do that?

I closed the back door, then picked up the two lemons near my feet, careful not to touch any glass, then reached for a third lemon that lay by the cabinet under the sink. I spotted another pop of yellow to my right, turned and reached for it, then whipped my hand back so fast I whacked it against the cabinet.

The lemon was half-hiding behind a shoe that stuck out from one corner of the island at an angle that told me it was still on somebody's foot. My heart launched into overdrive as I rounded the island.

I froze, unable to unlock my eyes from the wide unblinking ones of Willy Ellsworth, who was lying on his stomach with his head turned toward me. I dropped to my knees to check for a pulse, then bolted backwards when my eyes fell on the wooden knife handle protruding from his back.

I screamed loud enough to put Sonya Bean's bullhorn out of business.

Want to read more? *Pearl White Peril* is available now on Amazon!

A NOTE FROM EMILY

Thanks again for being a reader! I hope you enjoyed getting to know some of the characters in the Hadley Home Design Cozy Mystery series. Stay tuned because there are more books on the way!

If the Whisks and Whiskers Cat Café were a real place, you would find me there often, probably typing away on my laptop, enjoying a cup of coffee, or having brunch with friends and eating whatever yummy goodness was on the menu that day. I went to a cat cafe for the first time while living in Singapore, and I loved sipping on coffee in the company of cats. (Photos on my website!)

Darlington Hills is a fictional town, but it's located in Virginia near one of my favorite places in the United States: the Historic Triangle, which comprises Jamestown, Williamsburg, and York-town. Although I was born and raised in Texas, I have so many wonderful memories of traveling to Virginia to visit my grand-parents, aunts, uncles, and cousins.

Also, I love hearing from readers! You can find me on Face-book, Instagram, Pinterest, and Twitter at @obertonwrites. I share tidbits on all things related to my books, including links to my many sources of inspiration for this series, like recipes, interior design photos, and more.

You can also keep up with my latest books at emilyoberton.com and join my newsletter for exclusive subscriber deals, giveaways, and more. I'll also send you a free, printable travel brochure of the fictional town of Darlington Hills. It includes info on the town's history, legends, geographic information, recreational activities, and must-see attractions.

BONUS RECIPE!

Paw-some Brownie Raspberry Cheesecake

This delightful brownie raspberry cheesecake combines a rich, fudgy brownie base with a creamy cheesecake filling and is topped with a luscious raspberry swirl. Enjoy this indulgent treat with family and friends!

To download a pretty printable version of this recipe, join my newsletter at subscribepage.com/emilynewsletter.

Ingredients:

Raspberry Swirl
- 1 cup fresh or frozen raspberries
- 1/4 cup granulated sugar
- 1 tablespoon cornstarch
- 1 tablespoon water

Brownies
- 1 cup granulated sugar

- ½ cup packed brown sugar
- ½ cup powdered sugar
- ⅔ cup cocoa powder
- ¾ cup all-purpose flour
- ½ tsp sea salt
- 1 tsp baking powder
- ½ cup chocolate chips
- 2 large eggs
- 1 egg yolk
- ½ cup canola oil
- 2 Tbsp water
- ½ tsp vanilla extract

Cheesecake
- 16 oz cream cheese (softened)
- ¾ cup granulated sugar
- ½ cup whipped cream
- 2 large eggs
- 1 tsp vanilla extract

Instructions:

1. **Preheat oven** to 320ºF. Grease an 8 or 9-in springform pan with non-stick spray or butter.

2. **Raspberry Swirl:** In a small saucepan, combine the raspberries and sugar. Cook over medium heat, stirring occasionally, until the raspberries release their juices.

In a small bowl, mix the cornstarch and water, then add this mixture to the raspberry saucepan. Cook, stirring constantly, until the sauce thickens, about 2-3 minutes.

Remove from heat and strain the sauce through a fine-mesh sieve to remove seeds. Set aside to cool.

*Note: you can leave out the raspberry swirl steps to save time, and top the cheesecake with raspberries instead.

3. **Brownie base**: In one bowl, combine dry ingredients (granulated sugar, brown sugar, powdered sugar, cocoa powder, flour, sea salt, baking powder, and chocolate chips).

In another bowl, mix the eggs and egg yolk, canola oil, vanilla extract and water. Stir the dry mix into the wet mix until just combined (don't over-mix).

Pour into springform pan; spread it evenly with a spatula.

4. **Cheesecake filling:** Blend the softened cream cheese, whipped cream, sugar and vanilla. Add the eggs, stir into mixture. Spread evenly onto brownie mixture.

Pour the cheesecake filling over the baked brownie base, smoothing the top with a spatula. Drop spoonfuls of the raspberry sauce over the cheesecake filling.

Use a skewer or a knife to swirl the raspberry sauce into the cheesecake mixture, creating a marbled effect.

5. **Bake at 320° F** for 50-55 minutes or until a toothpick inserted into the middle of the cheesecake comes out clean.

Cool at room temperature for 1 hour, then place in refrigerator and cool 3 more hours or overnight to set.

Remove cheesecake from the springform pan, then garnish with raspberries, whipped cream, and drizzled chocolate sauce.

ACKNOWLEDGMENTS

My heart is full of gratitude for all of the encouragement I continuously receive along my writing journey. A special thanks to my husband, Miles, and children, Noelle and Landon, for cheering me on to the finish line (aka, that beautiful moment when I write THE END).

A million thank-yous to my mom, Muriel Dunn, for sharing her love of mystery books with me, beginning with the *Nancy Drew* series she gave me for Christmas when I was in elementary school. Thank you to Audrey Arnaud for her sweet encouragement to finish writing so she can read my next book, and to my editor, Cindy Davis, for her ever-brilliant edits and feedback on my books.

Thank you to all of my family and friends for your love and kindness. XO

ALSO BY EMILY OBERTON

Hadley Home Design Mystery Series

Book 1 - *Lemon Yellow Lies*

Book 2 - *Pearl White Peril*

Book 3 - *Berry Purple Betrayal*

Book 4 - *Cider Orange Chaos* - Coming soon!

ABOUT THE AUTHOR

Emily Oberton was born and raised in Houston, Texas. Since graduating from Texas A&M University, she has worked in news radio, corporate public relations, and as an independent PR consultant. In addition to writing cozy mysteries, she also enjoys decorating her own home (not just fictitious ones in Darlington Hills!), playing tennis, graphic design, and spending oodles of time with family and friends. Visit emilyoberton.com to learn more.

facebook.com/obertonwrites
instagram.com/obertonwrites
tiktok.com/@emilyobertonbooks

Made in the USA
Monee, IL
23 May 2023